T0209924

# CASSADA

Also by James Salter

# CASSADA
## JAMES SALTER

COUNTERPOINT · CALIFORNIA

Copyright © 2000 by James Salter

Library of Congress cataloging-in-publication data is available.

ISBN 978-1-61902-055-9

Text design by David Bullen Design
Cover design by Gerilyn Attebery
Cover photo courtesy of the author

COUNTERPOINT
Los Angeles and San Francisco, California
www.counterpointpress.com

*To the officers and men*
*and Norm Phillips*

FOREWORD

This novel about flying is drawn from another, earlier one, *The Arm of Flesh,* published in 1961 and largely a failure. It lay forgotten for a long time until Jack Shoemaker, the editor-in-chief of Counterpoint, suggested that it might be a companion piece to another book he had republished, *The Hunters,* which was my first novel.

I had revised *The Hunters* slightly for its second appearance. *The Arm of Flesh,* however, had serious faults and needed to be rewritten completely. Even the title deserved to be changed to, in this case, one of the principal characters. It may have been a mistake to try to stand on its feet again a failed book, but there were elements in it that continued to be interesting, among them the fact that it was sometimes the best along with the worst pilots who got killed for reasons the reader may come to understand, and that the group's acceptance of certain, sometimes very promising individuals is not always foregone or easy.

Beyond these things was the appeal of the period, the 1950s, barely a decade after the war; the place, the fighter bases of Europe; and the life itself. This new version, then, is meant to be the book the other might have been.

*July 2000*

# CASSADA

† † † † † † † † † †

Towards the end of the afternoon Dunning sat in the office, going through papers, from time to time licking a thumb as he turned a page. His broad brow was furrowed as he read, but he was an image of calm, like a judge examining briefs. Outside, the sky was dark, the clouds threatening rain. It had been that way since morning. From time to time in the stillness came the call of crows on the fenceposts or in bare branches at the edge of the field. Saturday late. Almost everyone gone.

A low sound, barely audible at first, made him turn his head. For a moment he seemed almost puzzled. The sound was faint but growing and unmistakable, like distant thunder. It was engines, wide open. They were as if headed towards him. He could hear them, full and unwavering, suddenly very close, almost overhead, roaring down the runway, low, but in the clouds. He never saw them. Then they had passed, but the sound stayed there, heavy and prophetic, before slowly fading, leaving silence behind. Dunning reached for the telephone, German like much of it, and dialed a number. Waiting for someone to answer he turned to the window again. It was absolutely quiet, the crows settled back in the trees. Impatiently he opened the thin directory to check the number when a voice said at last, "Base weather."

"Give me the forecaster," Dunning ordered.

"He's not here, suh."

"Where is he?"

"I doan know. He may be downstairs having coffee."

"Go and get him for me right away."

"Well, I don't know where he's at right now. Can I have him to call you?"

"No, goddamn it! Go get him! Go find him!"

"I'm not allowed to leave the weather station," the voice complained, almost sulkily.

"I don't give a damn what you're allowed to do. This is Major Dunning. Start finding him in a hurry!"

There was no reply, only faint breathing over the phone.

"Did you understand me?" Dunning said.

"Yes, suh."

"Then get me the forecaster!"

After a moment or two there was the sound of the phone laid down. Dunning tried to estimate the ceiling himself. He could just make out the control tower a mile away, the beacon on top of it turning steadily, vacant and pale, like the gaze of a blind man. There were dark, smokey patches of cloud near it floating nearly that low. He pushed the window open to hear better. Silence, even greater than it seemed before. Someone picked up the phone. The clearing of a throat.

"Forecaster speaking."

"Who is this?" Dunning demanded.

"Sergeant McEnerny, sir."

"Where the hell have you been? Aren't you supposed to be on duty?"

"Yes, sir," the sergeant said, "I am. I've been right here in the building all along."

"I'll find out where you've been, don't worry about that. What are you reporting the weather as? Someone just made a missed approach here."

"This is Major Dunning, sir?"

"That's right."

"I see, sir," the sergeant said. "Our latest observation is five hundred overcast," he was reading from a sheet of yellow paper, "and a mile and a half in light fog."

"When did you make that? Take a look out the window."

"The observation was made on the hour. That's exactly . . ." A pause. "Eighteen minutes ago."

"What does Spangdahlem have?" Dunning said. He could hear the movement on the other end, a clipboard being reached for.

"Let's see. They're calling it a little lower, Major. They're calling it three hundred broken."

"I thought so."

"Three hundred broken, five hundred overcast, one mile in fog."

"That sounds more like it."

"Well, sir, here we have five hundred and a mile and a half. That's current."

"Make another observation, sergeant," Dunning said, "and call me back. That's an order."

He was interrupted by the sound of footsteps. Someone was running down the hall. A head appeared in the doorway. Godchaux, one of the champions.

"Major?" There was something in his voice.

"What is it?" Dunning said, now quite alert.

"That was two of ours."

Dunning was the squadron commander, an exalted position. He was at the last command level of complete intimacy with all those beneath him, thirty-odd pilots and a hundred and forty men, some veterans, others serving in their unforgettable first unit, many he would have been able to call by their first name but he liked to use rank, roll it off his tongue, Sergeant somebody, Lieutenant. His mouth would purse oddly. He was a southerner; a strain of formality was in his blood.

He was well-known in the wing and even beyond. He was six years in grade, his wife, Mayann, a past president of the Officers' Wives Club. A command-wide list, confidential, requested by the Pentagon, had gone in from Twelfth Air Force. On it were the first twenty officers of the rank of major recommended regardless of seniority for promotion to lieutenant colonel. Davis R. Dunning, commander 44th Fighter Squadron, had been the first name. What had become of the list, what action would be taken, no one yet knew.

Isbell was his operations officer and right arm. A captain, he was a different sort, cool on the outside, cooler within with but one flaw: he was an idealist. Apart from that he had almost every thing necessary. He was experienced, confident, untiring. He had seven hundred hours in the airplane and two thousand besides, a hundred and sixty of them flying against the Russians and Chinese in Korea, fierce fights along the Yalu. In addition to other knowledge, he knew Dunning. They had been together for more than two years. They were, with the first sergeant, Banda, an ex-marine, triumvirs. All that was to be done or not to be done flowed from them.

Giebelstadt. It was entirely characteristic of Isbell to rise before daylight to check the alert flight. Early fall. The summer had been short, about one week instead of the usual two, as Dunning remarked. There was early frost turning the grass silver and flecking the airplane canopies with white. The cool smell of snow was already in the air together with the crowing of a distant rooster. Isbell walked down to the latrine in the darkness. The water was loud when he turned it on. He warmed his hands beneath it for a while. Cold was coming through the casement windows.

In their tent Dunning was still sleeping, heaped up like an old bear. It would be at least an hour before he woke, groaning and stretching his arms. He slept in his khaki underwear and sometimes received the first sergeant in it—it did not diminish his authority. He would go to the mess for coffee, talk a little to whoever was there, then wander over to the flight line.

Isbell had long since driven down the black road, heading into the open, past the trees beyond which like some mysterious stretch of water the silent runway lay. A wind was blowing, a German October wind, chilly, with points of moisture in it. They had been sent here on maneuvers, one lone runway, a building or two. There were stars in the sky and tug lights among the airplanes parked in a long line.

In the alert shack Ferguson was sitting by the stove, the poker dangling from his hands. A furious sound filled the room. It was coming from the stove which glowed brilliant red along the bottom, the middle of the lid, too, and the pipe. Outside, a stream of wild sparks was dancing above the dark roof.

"Step up and warm yourself, Chief," Ferguson invited. "Compliments of 'B' Flight."

"You'll be hot enough when that thing explodes."

"Have to chance that, Cap'n," Ferguson said. "The *Natchez* is trying to pass us."

"Which *Natchez*?"

"Right behind us, Cap'n. She's only half a mile back and gaining all the time."

"You'd better cut down the draft," Isbell said.

Ferguson raised a boot and kicked the hinged door closed a little.

On the floor lay a page of the *Stars and Stripes* he had been piercing with the radiant tip of the poker. There was a full-length picture of a girl in a bathing suit. Only her head and shoulders were untouched.

"What time do you go on status?" Isbell asked.

"In about five minutes."

Just as he said it, the scramble phone rang. A line check. As Ferguson was hanging up, the others began to come in, rubbing their hands and going to the stove. Godchaux was last. He was twenty and had been in the squadron for more than a year, Dunning's favorite, "the best natural pilot I ever saw." Isbell didn't disagree. White teeth and the smile of an angel. Show me a man who knows how to lie, he thought, and I'll show you a smile of genuine beauty, I'll show you someone who knows how the world runs.

Godchaux stood with his back to the stove and his elbows out to the side, espaliered against the glow, almost satanic. Isbell beckoned him with a slight lifting of the chin.

"Yes, sir," Godchaux responded without moving.

Isbell motioned to him. Godchaux took a step or two forward.

"Did you have a flashlight out there?"

Godchaux's innocence held for a moment and then he shook his head, not much, like a mischievous, already forgiven boy.

"How'd you inspect the airplane, then?" Isbell said.

"I borrowed the crew chief's."

"You did, eh? Where's yours? What's wrong, don't you have one of your own?"

"Yes, sir."

"Where is it?"

"The batteries are no good, Captain. They're dead."

"Well, buy some," Isbell said. "You're getting paid enough."

"Yes, sir."

"Today."

Grace, the commander of "B" Flight, was shaking his head a little in fatherly disappointment, as if agreeing. In all likelihood he had no flashlight himself.

Soon after, there was the uneven ring of the field phone and the first scramble went off, two ships flowing down the runway, fleeing from a roar that washed over the field like a furnace thrown open, making the corrugated walls tremble. Isbell stood watching as they crossed the trees together, the wheels coming up. An hour of absolution in the clean, holy morning. An hour and a half. How often he had relied upon it himself, a taste of the immaculate with unknown cities far below and in cold silence the first mist vanishing from the hills.

Dunning came to the pilots' meeting later. He appeared in the doorway a few minutes before eight o'clock as someone was trying to go out and stood there, filling the whole frame, waiting for them to come to their senses and step aside. He was the size of a lineman and in fact had played two years in college early in the war. He'd had his crew chief remove the spacer from the back of the seat. As a result it was hard to fly his airplane. It was like sitting up in bed.

"What do you think of that bird of mine?" he would say.

"Yes, sir. It's all right."

"A little slow," Godchaux said.

"Slow? Slow? You're crazy. It's the fastest ship on the line."

"If you say so, Major."

"Don't just take my word for it."

"It may not be fast, but it is roomy."

"What's that supposed to mean?"

"You can hardly reach the stick. You have to have arms like a gorilla."

"You've got to grow some, that's all," Dunning said. He looked around, grinning.

There were always a couple of minutes like that. Nothing began until Dunning leaned back with an expectant look on his face and puffed on his cigar. He would listen attentively, hands folded one over the other in his lap, thumbs like broom handles. After Isbell finished he would rise to say a few words himself, walking to the front like an owner, hands in the pockets of his flying suit. He started off with a courtly, "Gentlemen. I'd like to impress a few things on your minds," he said, "though we may have mentioned them before. Very important things. This field, gentlemen, pretty as it is, has a few shortcomings which you should all be aware of. Can you name one of them, Lieutenant Godchaux?"

"No GCA," Godchaux said.

"No GCA, gentlemen. If the weather starts closing in, don't take any chances, there's no one here to talk you down. What else, Lieutenant Grace?"

"The runway is a thousand feet shorter than ours, sir."

"Shorter runway. Also unfamiliar. The road you always put your base leg over back home—you know the one I mean—it's not here. You have to use your judgement more in the landing pattern. Short and unfamiliar. Got that? Lieutenant Ferguson, what else?"

In a slow voice, "Long way to town," Ferguson said.

Amid the laughter someone said, "But when you get there . . ."

"Good beer," Ferguson added.

"Nice professional attitude," Dunning said, perhaps tolerantly, it was difficult to tell.

When the meeting was over a small circle formed. Harlan, blunt and usually suspicious, began on the inevitable subject, flying time and how much a rival squadron, the 72nd, was getting. They had over five hundred hours already this month. They were pushing. "They say Pine claims he's going to get twelve hundred."

Dunning smiled at him, a false V, nothing humorous in it, just a seam across his face like the line on a stuffed toy. Harlan shrugged slightly.

"That's what I hear."

"I wouldn't pay too much attention to that," Dunning said knowledgeably. "There just may be a few things Captain Pine doesn't know about."

"That's the trouble," Harlan muttered. He was a country boy. His hands were large, too. "He don't know, so he'll probably go ahead and fly the twelve hundred."

Dunning nodded a bit as if weighing. "I wouldn't worry about that, Lieutenant," he said.

Dunning's squadron was the red tails. He would never admit to fearing anything from the yellows. Pine was famous for the conviction that flying hours were the magic formula: "Log two hours every flight whether you fly that long or not." Isbell was more constrained. There was the meaning of a signature, an official statement.

"Some of them got over twenty hours apiece already," Harlan said though Dunning had gone. "I know that for sure."

The scramble phone rang. The two alert pilots were already out the door and running across the grass by the time the horn began. Isbell was looking at his watch. It seemed a long time before the engines started. Then came a great swelling of sound as the ships pulled out and started down the taxiway, moving fast. Gradually quiet returned. About a minute later they could be heard taking off.

"Just the same, I bet they get twelve hundred," Harlan was saying. "They always get a lot of time. Maybe they don't brief so much."

All that morning there were scrambles, four or five at least. "B" Flight was in luck. There were days when the phone never rang. Wickenden, the "A" Flight commander, had drawn up a chart to show how his flight had had four days of bad weather since they'd been there and Grace's flight none; they were getting all the time, he complained.

"It'll average out," Isbell told him.

"It never does," Wickenden said. He had Phipps who'd joined at the same time as Godchaux and they'd come from flying school together. Godchaux now had almost a hundred hours more.

"Why is that?" Isbell said.

"He's in Grace's flight. Grace is like Pine. You know that."

"I don't think so," Isbell said.

At midday, silvery and slow, the courier floated down the final approach and then skimmed for a long time near the ground getting ready to touch. Nose pointed high, it taxied in. Phipps went to meet it. He stood off to one side and watched it swing around, the grass quivering behind and pebble shooting off the concrete. When the engines died he walked up and waited for the door to open. There was mail, spare parts, and one passenger, a second lieutenant wearing an overcoat. His baggage was handed down. It turned out he was joining the squadron. "This is the 44th, right?"

"Yeah, this is it. Well, you're lucky."

"What do you mean?"

"Nothing," Phipps said. "It's just what they told me."

The new man's name was Cassada. He was Phipps's height with hair a little fairer and combed back, Anglo style. Phipps helped him carry his bags while being careful not to be too responsive to questions. Cassada was looking around as they walked. Were these their planes, he wanted to know? Were pilots assigned a plane? Were their names painted on them? Phipps answered yes.

"I'll take you over to meet Captain Isbell," he said.

"Is he the squadron commander?"

"Who, Captain Isbell? No, he's ops."

"Oh," Cassada said.

He was just out of flying school but he'd served as an enlisted man for two years before. He didn't look that old.

In the mess they found both the major and Isbell. Phipps presented the new man.

"Cassada," the major repeated as if remembering the name.

"Yes, sir." There were unfamiliar faces all around.

"That's a pretty famous name," Dunning said. "You don't happen to have anyone in your family who's been in the service?"

"Just my uncle, sir."

Dunning stopped chewing. "Your uncle? That's not the general, by any chance?"

"No, sir. He was only a private."

"You're no relation to the general?"

"No, sir. That's QUE, I think. My name is spelled CASS."

"CASS."

"Cassada."

Dunning resumed eating. "Did you just get in?"

"He just got in on the courier," Phipps said.

"I was talking to Lieutenant Cassada, here."

"Yes, sir."

"Have you had your lunch?"

"No, sir."

"Go ahead through the line and then come on back," Dunning said.

While Cassada was eating, Dunning asked him a number of questions, where he'd gone to flying school, how much time he had, where he was from, but in fact he listened carefully to only one or two of the answers. He was telling Cassada what an outstanding squadron he had joined, picking his teeth as he spoke. He seemed unobservant. He relied on strong instinct, deciding right off if a man could cut it or not. In the case of Cassada who had not said a lot, perhaps a dozen words, Dunning was not much impressed. He liked second lieutenants who reminded him of himself when he was one. Roaring. Full of hell, like Baysinger who had a wide gap between his front teeth and one night in the club, just as drunk as Dunning, got into a wrestling match with him and broke his leg. Baysinger had long since completed his tour and was gone, as were the crutches that Dunning hobbled around on for two months afterwards.

Dunning had on a wool shirt, a green tie, and a tweed jacket. Shaking some tonic on his hair, he combed it down. A damp towel hung at the foot of the bed. He took it and cleaned his shoes. He looked like a farmer, a corn-fed farmer on a Saturday night. As a final touch he stuffed a khaki handkerchief in his breast pocket and a thick wallet, folded double, into the back pocket of his pants.

"Might turn out to be a real whoop-de-do," he commented to Isbell.

There was a drab *gasthaus* on the long road of trees that led to town. Dunning had gotten to know the woman who ran it well enough to slap her familiarly on the behind and tell her to bring whatever it was, a *prima* schnitzel or some good, none of that cheap stuff, wine. He knew a little German. He could say something tasted like rat poison, which always brought a laugh.

A cheer went up when he and Isbell entered. Everybody was there or had better be, even the armament and communications officers. All four flight commanders, not sitting together but sown among the rest, Wickenden, Grace, Reeves, and Cunati, who had false front teeth, their history unknown. Isbell sat down beside Harlan who was debunking something, as usual, in this case the war which had been over for a decade. He didn't know that much about it, he admitted, picking at the wet label on a bottle, but he knew one thing: we should never of got involved. It was never our business. His pale blue eyes watched what his fingers were doing. It didn't do us a bit of good.

Grace had a different view: it was all part of a bigger fight.

"What bigger fight?"

"Against communism. The Germans were really helping us."

"You mean they were on our side?"

"In a way."

"That's news to me."

"A lot of things are," Grace said.

"Oh, yeah?" Harlan turned his head. "What do you say, Captain?"

"I think it's about even."

"What do you mean, even?"

"Neither of you know what you're talking about."

"Aw, don't try to flatter us."

"Gee, that's a big word for you," Grace said.

It was Friday night, the night for drinking. It would go on for hours. Isbell sat, not really listening, his gaze moving over the crowd, casual but searching, he was not sure for what. True comrades perhaps. Even friends.

Reeves, he thought, looking at him, unknowable, really. Wickenden. He hesitated there. Wickenden's round head, hair cut close, shaved like a Russian's, the scalp gleaming through. He was talking about something, the new velocities, the tremendous shocking power. Even a gut shot would bring them down now—shatter their nervous system. He didn't approve of that. His mouth tightened.

Too much power, it took the sport out of it. You ought to have to hit them in a spot the size of a plum. Right in the brainpan. The heart. Or lose them. "Give the beast a chance."

It was a cold night. Across the dim field Isbell could make out some kind of animal moving. Then he could see it, a *hirsch* that hadn't presented a very good target, drifting through the black woods, its fine head and antlers. There was a splintering frost. The *hirsch* was stepping slim-legged through it, unsteadily but with a matchless grace, stopping every couple of yards while his stomach filled with blood. The sides of his body were wet with it, heaving gently, and something was behind him, trailing him in the dark. This way! Something was crashing through stiff branches. The *hirsch*, feeling for the one time ever a terrible dizziness, begins to move faster, in panic. The twigs are exploding. Over here! This way!

Who among them, then, Isbell wondered, someone nearly over-looked, silent and reflective, or another, arguing and intense? God-chaux—he was what it was all about. Grace. The best pilots. Across the room, wedged between men he did not know, was the new one. Fair hair, eyebrows almost joined in the middle. Never trust a man when they come together, they say. As good a rule as any, and the new man, taking it all in, just beginning to select a few idols, Isbell could have picked them out himself, the false glitter.

He emptied his glass and raised a finger for another. It was curi-ous. There were times when he could see them in an entirely differ-ent way, for what they were, full of simple courage and youth. God-chaux had a smile that even death would not erase. Dumfries, that idiot, smooth-cheeked and smiling, he had something, too, decent and admirable. There were times when Isbell trusted them all. They were bound together, all of them, he and Dunning too in a great orbit, coming deceptively close to the rest of life and then swinging away. At the extremities were North Africa where they went for gunnery once or twice a year and at the other end the skies of England where great mock battles were sometimes fought. The rest was at home in the Rhineland, rumor, routine, occasional deployments, Munich now and then. They toured the Western world together, stopping at Rome to refuel. Socked in? Divert to Naples—watch the olive trees if you land to the west. Something was usually beginning before the last thing ended. Isbell's true task was biblical. It was the task of Moses—he would take them to within sight of what was promised, but no further. To the friezes of heaven, which nobody knew were there.

Dunning was drinking coffee and talking to a couple of the crew chiefs. Godchaux and Phipps sat down nearby. It was a cloudy morning. The last flights were landing.

When the crew chiefs had gone, Dunning turned. He examined Godchaux for a moment.

"Mighty sporty today, aren't we?"

"Sir?"

"Just what are they," Dunning asked looking towards Godchaux's feet, "the new Air Force regulation?"

"What's that, sir?"

"I was under the impression we'd all pretty well agreed on a color."

"Oh, you mean these." It was a pair of red socks. "I guess I wasn't paying much attention. I figured the flying suit covered them anyway. I guess I should change them."

"I would suggest that you do, Lieutenant."

Phipps, looking towards Godchaux, was making a darting motion with his eyes.

"Right now, do you mean?" Godchaux asked Dunning.

"Just as soon as possible."

Godchaux saw it then, the thin band of green and black argyle.

"Yes, sir," he said.

"Well?" Dunning said. Godchaux hadn't moved.

"Sir, can I borrow your jeep?"

"No."

Godchaux stood up.

"Sit down," Dunning said, not looking at him.

"I'll change them when I go back at noon," Godchaux said. "There's just one thing . . ."

"What's that?"

"Do you want me to bring you back a pair, too?"

Phipps smothered a laugh. Dunning stared disapprovingly at him, as at someone who had asked a stupid question. "What's bothering you?"

"Nothing, sir," Phipps said, still believing he was part of the fun. Then he lost confidence and changed his expression. He looked embarrassed. He rubbed the tip of his nose nervously. The commander's moods were unpredictable, the burly figure who had led fighter-bomber missions in Korea, rail cuts far to the north, coming back afterwards, spent and dark with sweat. Dunning didn't talk about it, he didn't have to. It was part of his aura.

Cassada came along then, alone, wearing a flight jacket that was too large for him. The sleeves nearly touched his knuckles. He saw Dunning gesture and sat down. How was he making out? Dunning wanted to know. Fine, Cassada said.

"Has Captain Isbell assigned you to anybody for your checkout yet?"

"Yes, sir. Lieutenant Grace."

"Good. You'll be in good hands. How about a cup of coffee?"

"No, thank you."

"What's wrong? Don't you drink coffee?"

"No, sir."

"I never heard of a fighter pilot who wouldn't drink coffee. What is it, part of your religion or something?"

"It's the caffeine, Major. I seem to be sensitive to the caffeine."

"What *do* you drink?"

"Well, tea sometimes, sir."

"Tea?"

Ferguson drank coffee. In fact his need for it was pressing. He had landed a few minutes before and had flown with a hangover. The lines imprinted from the oxygen mask were still on his face.

"Feeling all right there?" Dunning asked.

Ferguson was holding the cup in both, almost trembling, hands.

"You look a little pale," Dunning went on.

"No, sir, Major. I feel fine."

"Town last night?"

"No, sir, it's just a little sinus up here," he touched the bridge of his nose, "that's all."

"Maybe you need some tea."

"Sir?"

"Tea," the major said.

Ferguson, large and somewhat aimless, was puzzled. Something he had missed. "I don't think so," he said glancing around. There was something going on.

When Dunning had gone, Ferguson said, "What was all that about?"

"Ask Cassada."

"I just said I didn't drink coffee. The caffeine," Cassada said.

"He never met a fighter pilot who didn't drink coffee," Phipps said.

"I hope you like beer," Godchaux said.

In the darkness Cassada woke, cold German night outside. It was just past five. The day he had been waiting for was at hand. He wondered what the weather was; it had been clear the night before, stars in a strange heaven. He lay quietly, unable to sleep, going over various possibilities, those he might soon have to face.

He went to breakfast and sat with others but said nothing. He was still not accepted. This day would begin to change that. He was impatient for it. Afterwards things would be different.

Grace met him in operations. Their airplanes had already been assigned. Cassada's eyes several times went to the numbers written in grease pencil on the scheduling board. Outside, the planes themselves, heavy black cables plugged into them, stood on the ramp.

They went over the emergency procedures: fire warning light, electrical failure, flameout. There was a power unit just outside making a racket. In the next room the operations clerks were using the adding machine. Godchaux and some others were playing hearts. "Smoke the old bitch," they were crying. "Smoke her out."

"What if both hydraulic systems go out?" Cassada wanted to know.

"That's bad," Grace said.

"Can you move the controls at all?"

Grace shook his head. He had a broad, smooth face and close-cropped hair.

"Not even using the trim?"

"No," Grace said.

Hearts was the game of choice. It showed your true character. Godchaux had the lead, the last trick lay faceup in front of him. Two hearts had fallen in it, the ace and nine. It was Harlan's ace. Ferguson was chanting, "Smoke, smoke."

"Shooting?" Harlan asked.

"Yeah, sure I am," Godchaux said. He tapped his fingers on the back of his cards.

"Well, is there anything else you can do?" Cassada wanted to know. He had confidence in Grace. He was in no position not to have, but still. "Can you do anything?"

"That's what you carry a small screwdriver for," Grace said. "You have one, don't you?"

"No."

"You'd better get one before we go up."

"You mean you can do something in the cockpit?"

"That's right. You unscrew the clock."

"The clock?"

"For a souvenir. Just put it in your pocket and bail out."

Cassada was uncertain whether or not to smile.

"Now, if something happens up there while we're flying along," Grace said, "and you hear me tell you: 'Forget the clock,' you know what that means."

Cassada nodded numbly. He heard a puff of laughter from the hearts game. His face was already red.

"It means get out right now," Grace said. "Don't wait. Go without it."

They began to review the mission card after that. Cassada had made up his mind about Grace. He admired him.

"I forget what's been played, it's been so long," Harlan was complaining. As it happened, he had the spade queen. He never passed it unless there was no choice. He was hard to beat. He nearly always passed diamonds or the ace or king of spades.

Outside the sun was up and the sky pale blue. After he had inspected his own ship, Grace walked over to Cassada's and stood partly on the wing to supervise the start. Cassada hit the start switch. The rising whine began and then the full flow of sound, solid, deeper, as the engine swelled to life.

"That's good!" Grace shouted.

Cassada, intent on the instruments, watched the various needles that had suddenly, ominous as serpents, raised their heads. He felt a tap on his shoulder.

"That's good!" Grace cried close to his ear. "I'm going to mine now."

With that, he jumped down and went quickly to his plane. As he was strapping himself in he looked over at Cassada whose head was turned in his direction, like a dog told to stay. It was a beautiful morning, sunlight, good visibility. Grace started his engine. He motioned for the power cables to be pulled and on the radio said, "Fortify Black Lead."

"Black Two," came the prompt reply.

"Go ahead, call the tower."

Cassada tried, but there was no answer. He tried a second time and a third. Then, as if uncertain, he waited.

"You might try them on tower frequency," Grace said. He could see Cassada, after a moment's hesitation, bend down to see what channel he was on.

"Black, go Channel One," Cassada finally said.

"That's better."

They had no further trouble. Grace behind, they taxied out. Many eyes were on them casually, some like Isbell's, attentive. Together the planes lined up on the runway, black smoke mounting behind them, and then the first plane began to roll, slowly at first, then faster, Grace, in the chase plane, close behind. The powerful sound, as thick as if it were metal, lay over everything.

Grace, responsible for the supervision on this first flight, watched the arrowy shape in front of him lift and leave the ground with a slight unsteadiness. He saw the gear retract, the flaps, and the speed increase. He was connected to the plane ahead by a single filament finer than silk and no stronger: the invisible link that carried his voice. Usually he said little. There were pilots who, like women, talked a lot on the radio, but Grace said only what was necessary. He was highly regarded as a pilot and as the only flight commander below the rank of captain. He watched as Cassada climbed and at altitude began the stalls. Straight ahead, in a left turn, a right. Then the steep turns. Whatever the card said—there was not much on that first one.

Grace was flying off to the side and began a gradual turn away when Cassada had finished. "OK, join up, Black Two," he said.

He watched as the other plane, closing too fast, swept above him, banking steeply. Its speed brakes came out. Grace continued a gentle turn. The other plane had dropped back and hung there on the inside, trying to cut him off. It took a long time. Grace saw what the trouble was. "Speed brakes," he called.

They were pulled in right away. A few moments later, not to Grace's surprise, Cassada went sailing past.

"Settle down," Grace said.

Finally Cassada came into close formation. Grace let him establish himself and then began a turn, and another. Cassada stayed in position. Grace made them steeper. Eventually they were vertical, even beyond. Then he pulled up so Cassada was looking into the sun and held it there while the airspeed drained away. He rolled onto one wing and headed down. At about five hundred knots he began a hard turn, steady and solid. Cassada stayed in close.

"Let's try some trail," Grace said.

He watched as Cassada dropped back and swung in behind.

"Closer. About half a ship-length."

He was looking up into the rear-view mirror, and after some moments Cassada's wingtips appeared which meant he was in the right position, but then they fell away. He waited until they returned, easing back in, not too steady but remaining there. Watching them he made a turn, first one way, then the other, then pulled the nose up and did a roll. The wingtips were visible until just at the end. They vanished but came quickly back. Grace did the same thing again, making the turns faster. The wingtips bobbed but stayed in sight.

In Grace could be found all the qualities desired in a flight commander, or almost all. He was levelheaded and able and judged the men around him by a single standard, so simple it was sublime: could they fly? He did not put himself above them save in this one regard. It was the one thing that mattered.

He had almost forgotten who he was flying with. He dropped the nose and let it build up speed. The wingtips were jerking. Grace pulled up sharply and continued, straight up, onto his back. Just past the top of the loop, as he expected, the ship behind him fell back. He finished the loop and waited for Cassada to move in again. Then he did another. It was about the same. He rocked his wings and waited. Cassada slid to the side and slowly pulled into close formation. Grace said,

"How much fuel do you have?"

The reply was garbled. He asked a second time. He heard, "Twelve hundred pounds."

"Go ahead and practice your landing pattern," Grace instructed.

At ten thousand feet, well above the ground, Cassada did two of them. They looked good.

"All right, take us back to the field," Grace said.

They were to the south of it. Cassada first headed west but soon corrected. With Grace trailing behind, he found the field and entered the pattern and instead of landing made the required go-around, requesting closed traffic.

"You're cleared for closed pattern and landing," the tower replied.

One after the other the two planes came down and landed. Isbell was watching from mobile control. He drove in to talk to Grace afterwards.

"The landing was good," he said. "How was he in the air?"

"Not too bad."

"No difficulties? Nothing dangerous?"

"No. He'll be all right, I think. I'll take him."

"We haven't decided about that," Isbell said. "Where is he, anyway?"

Someone came around the side of Maintenance, arms held out oddly like a shirt on a clothesline. The flying suit, clinging and wet, was sheathed against his legs and chest. It was Cassada. He'd gotten sick to his stomach while in the air and in the midst of things had thrown up, catching it in one of his flying gloves but afterwards it spilled. He'd been in the latrine trying to wash himself off, but the smell was still there.

"What happened?" Grace said.

"I'm OK."

"Go on back to the quarters and change," Isbell said.

"I'm all right," Cassada repeated. His face was grey.

"I'll fill out a card," Grace said. "There's not that much to say. It's an easy flight. You waited a little too long after takeoff, let the airspeed build too much before you began your climb. Do you have any comments?"

Cassada's teeth had begun to chatter lightly in the cold.

"What a great plane," he said with enthusiasm. "It really is! When you were doing those rolls it was just so smooth. I know I was a little ragged . . ."

"Rolls?" Isbell said. There was silence. "For Christ's sake, Grace."

Grace looked at the ground and rubbed the tip of his nose with a thumb.

"Did you offer to help the crew chief clean up the cockpit?" Isbell said to Cassada. "Better go do that."

Cassada said, "Yes, sir."

When he had gone, Isbell said, "Bob."

"Yes, sir."

"I had more confidence in you than that."

"Yes, sir."

"Do you know what I expect of you?"

"Yes."

"No, you don't. If you knew, you'd never do a stupid thing like that. What do you know about whether this man can fly or not? You don't. That's what the transition missions are for. If the major found out about this he'd take away your flight."

"Captain, I'm sorry. It wasn't good judgement. He seemed to be doing pretty well and I just got carried away."

"You don't understand something."

Grace did not reply.

"I trust you," Isbell said. "I trust you will do the right thing. Don't make me think I've made a mistake."

"No, sir."

"I'm not going to say anything to the major. You better make sure nobody else does."

Cassada was carrying a bucket of water towards the parked planes when Grace caught up with him.

"Hey!"

Cassada stopped. "Gee, I'm sorry," he said. He sneezed. "I didn't realize what I was saying."

"The next time don't just blurt out the first thing that comes to you."

"I'm really sorry," Cassada said again. His hair was wet and lying flat.

"Another thing. Don't mention this. I mean that. To nobody. We'll both be out of here."

"Yes, sir. I mean, OK."

There was already a bond.

In the mess Wickenden sat smoking a cigarette after breakfast, his habit. He had others, all well defined like the clapping of the top of his Zippo lighter, opening it and clapping it shut again a number of times, a sort of overture before he spoke. The lighter was from his old squadron, the case enameled in yellow and black squares. Now that was a squadron, the display of it seemed to say, the yellow and black checkered squadron, and he was like a spider, waiting for the tremor that would be one of them asking about it.

He had a firm jaw and the fate of having been born in the wrong century. The cavalry was what he was made for, riding in the dust of the Mexican border with cracked lips and a line edged into his hair from the strap of a campaign hat. Even at that he would have been longing for the old days.

He sat by himself, the tray in front of him. Wick the prick. You can give them all haircuts, he liked to say, teach them to salute, and call them gentlemen, but what does that mean? Good pay, the best equipment in the world, and with all that they still have the guts to complain. What are they getting out of the Air Force they want to know? Their cavities filled for one thing.

At the next table he could see the squadron commander, what passed for one, looking fatherly and listening to what had happened the night before at some bar. The ones who weren't married chasing after waitresses. Sirens, to hear them talk. Goddesses, skin like milk. Ferguson was one of them. And Godchaux, naturally.

Then, hair bent the wrong way from sleeping on it, in came the new man. He went through the food line and found a place to sit. Head bent forward, he began to eat.

"I like to see my pilots putting away a good breakfast," Dunning commented.

Cassada, unaware, kept eating and as he did, smoothed his hair.

"Ah, Lieutenant Cassada," Dunning said.

Cassada's head came up. "Sir?"

"I said I like to see my pilots eat a good breakfast before they go up. But in your case I don't know."

There were some snickers.

"Are you scheduled to fly again this morning?"

"Yes, sir."

"Maybe you'd better just have some coffee then. Oh, I forgot. Tea."

Cassada tried to smile. He wasn't sure whether or not to stop eating.

Wickenden, sitting alone, watched it all. They'd turn him into a fighter pilot, all right. If he had the stuff. He'd walk into the briefing room one day like the rest of them with a rolled-up newspaper in his back pocket and picking his teeth. Gentlemen all and the world's best.

"Go ahead and finish your breakfast," Isbell said when the major had gone. "He was only pulling your leg."

"I'm . . . it's OK," Cassada said.

"Go ahead and have your breakfast."

Cassada looked at him for a moment with a cool, unbothered eye. Then he looked away.

"That's all right, Captain," he said.

Wickenden saw it clearly. More than clearly. He could see right through this one.

The first Saturday night after coming home there was a party at the club. Nearly everyone came. Mayann Dunning was sitting at the bar when Dumfries and his wife in what looked like her communion dress came in. They were almost the last ones and wandered along the big table trying to decide which places were taken.

"We're late," Dumfries said to Mayann. "Where is everybody?"

"In the other room."

"What's going on?"

"Yes, what's happening?" Laurie asked in a little voice.

"They got a new singer while you were away," Mayann said. "At least that's what she's supposed to be."

"Aren't you going in?" Dumfries asked.

"No, I've already seen her."

"I guess I'll have a look."

"Where are you going?" Laurie asked.

"I'll be right back."

"We just got here."

"Let him go," Mayann said. "You wouldn't want him to miss it, would you?"

She and Dunning had met in college. She was, at the time, grey-eyed and unknowable though not shy. She was the daughter of a pharmacist and had been given the combined name of both grandmothers. She had inherited, in addition, her mother's outspokenness, one might even say boldness. It was known that she had remarked of the wing commander's wife that she would be a wonderful woman if she ever told the truth. Had this reached the wrong ears it could have been damaging. Some things are unpardonable but Mayann was bored.

She should have been born a man, she often felt, been one of them instead of talking all the time about how terrible the maids were and why didn't they shave under their arms. She should have had hard legs to swagger on and slim hips.

Laurie had resigned herself to sitting with Mrs. Dunning who she felt looked down on her somehow although it should have been the other way around, the things you heard. It was not long before the music stopped and everyone began coming back in. Two drinks in one hand and a cigar in the other, wearing a string tie and an expression of amusement, Dunning came to the bar. He set one of the drinks, the ice in it nearly melted, in front of his wife.

"Did you get enough of it?" she said.

"Ho, ho," he said.

"What does that mean?"

"She's too much for any of these boys."

"Well, that rules you out."

Dunning only smiled.

Marian Isbell, coming up behind him, was irritated. They had been away for a whole month, she complained, and when they finally got back some *fraulein* was all they were interested in.

"Tommy find that interesting?" Mayann said.

"You'd think they had more sense than to hire a girl like that."

"I don't think they hired her."

"What do you mean?"

"She's with the band."

"You should have seen Ferguson. He certainly was sitting up all of a sudden."

Isbell joined them.

"Marian says she likes the singer," Mayann said.

"Ferguson likes her."

"Don't lay it all on Ferguson," Marian said.

"He's apparently more interested in music than we knew."

"Lieutenant Ferguson!" Dunning called. Ferguson had just come back in the room.

"All present, sir!"

"Come over here a minute."

"Yes, sir."

"I was just wondering . . . What do you think of this new singer?"

Ferguson made a sound like the growl of a cat.

"I thought so. What is it exactly you like?"

"The dress," Ferguson said.

"What about it?"

"Do you think she's wearing anything under it?" he said.

"She couldn't be," Mayann said.

"You think so?"

"There isn't any room."

"I was under the impression you liked her voice," Dunning went on.

"Oh, yes," Ferguson said. "That, too."

He was the first one to go back when the band struck up again. The club steward meanwhile opened a dividing curtain that had been drawn between the two rooms. Those sitting at the table could now see. The singer, in a white dress with a little fringe at the bosom and hips, had walked up the three steps to the stage and its brilliant bath of light.

Godchaux, lingering behind, came to the bar.

"Enjoying yourself?" Mayann asked.

Godchaux gave a slight shrug. His face always wore a guileless expression.

"Do you want a drink?"

She called the bartender.

"Yes, Mrs. Dunning?" He was looking towards the stage. The singer was in the spotlight, her mouth near the microphone, the little fringe at the top trembling as she breathed.

"You're too old for that, Hans. Give us a couple of drinks," Mayann said.

He reached down for the glasses. "She's *prima*, no?"

"Do you know where she's from?" Godchaux asked.

"What's that, Lieutenant?"

"Where's she from?"

"Munich," Hans said.

"That figures."

"What would you like to drink?"

"Bourbon."

"With water?"

"On the rocks."

"Mrs. Dunning?"

"Give me another of these." She pushed forward her nearly empty glass, ignoring the one her husband had left for her. To Godchaux she said, "How come you're not in there with the rest of them straining your eyes?"

"Oh . . ."

"What is it, you already have a girlfriend?"

"Me?" Godchaux said. "Uh, not really. Not here. In Munich . . ."

"I see. So how do you handle it? Don't you get horny?"

The smile, always ready to appear on Godchaux's face, did, but it was embarrassed. He glanced at the floor.

"Well, don't you?"

"I, uh . . . To be honest, I'm not used to talking like this."

"With a woman?"

"I guess so."

"Your face is all red."

Something was occurring, perhaps it was occurring. He knew he was in good favor with the squadron commander; he had never thought beyond that. They drank for a while in silence and watched the singer. After the set was over, Ferguson brought her back with him. She was no less impressive at close hand.

"They want me to be drunk," she said to Mayann. She held up a glass dark with whiskey.

"Can't think what for," Mayann said.

"Oh, ho," the singer said, smiling.

Ferguson was on one side of her, Harlan on the other. They were asking her where in Munich she was from, what part? Someone started singing *In München steht ein Hofbräuhaus* and without much urging she joined in. Cassada had his glass raised high and was singing without knowing the words. He was watching their mouths and getting one every now and then.

"It's nice having them back, isn't it?" Jackie Grace said.

"What?"

"It's nice having them back."

"I don't know," Mayann said. "Sometimes I think I might like somebody else back."

For a moment it was not understood. Then,

"Oh, Mayann. You!"

"Don't you ever feel that way?"

"Oh, Mayann. Goodness!"

Ferguson had jumped up to make room for a waiter with a tray-
ful of glasses and German champagne. "Put it right here," he said.

"What's all that for?" Harlan asked.

"Nothing," Ferguson said. "Just champagne. A celebration."

He was passing the bottles around to be opened. When the first
cork popped there was a spurt that went across the table. Mayann
jumped back.

"You idiot," she said.

Cassada was holding a bottle by the neck, foam pouring over his
hand. Standing up straight then, unsteady, "Oh, I'm sorry," he said.

"What's the matter with you?" The front of her dress was wet.
She was holding it away from herself.

Cassada had come around the table and offered her his handkerchief. "Here, use this, Mrs. Dunning."

"You use it."

With the handkerchief still folded in a square, he bent down and
began stroking. Mayann held her dress taut.

"Just stick to the wet spots," she said. She could see him blush.
He looked up.

"I'm really sorry, Mrs. Dunning. Can I pay to have it cleaned?"

She disregarded this.

"Can I get you a glass of champagne?" he asked.

"Instead of just pouring it on me, you mean?"

He didn't know what to say. "I'm really sorry."

He held the bottle in both hands while he poured, the bottom
against his stomach. "Here you are," he said politely.

The champagne made it a party. Lank-haired and whispering Ferguson was inviting the singer to ride into town with him on his
motorcycle after the band finished. Harlan was talking to her, too.
The gleam of her bare shoulders was drawing them to her, the
white dress. The bachelors were in their glory. They were standing
against the wall, singing and spilling champagne over themselves,

shaking the bottle with a thumb over the top and then spraying it around, faces wet as swimmers'. The singing got louder and cruder. The bar closed but nobody left. Finally the club officer came by.

"It's all right," Dunning told him with a confident air.

"Certainly, Major," the club officer said. He just wanted them to watch out for the furniture.

"We're not going to hurt it," somebody said.

They were certainly spilling enough champagne, the club officer remarked.

"Ahh," Cassada muttered, "so that's where it's going."

Dunning, undisturbed by the incident of the champagne, put an arm around Cassada's shoulders. The singer was gone. She had sneaked out after the final number with a bandsman's coat around her. "Well, how do you like the squadron, son?"

"I guess I like it fine."

"You *guess*? What the hell! Don't you know you are in the best goddamn squadron in the Air Force. You *guess*? Let me tell you something, people would kill to be in the spot you're in. The best squadron and the best planes. Captain Isbell!" he called. "Who the hell is this man?"

"He's a new lieutenant we've got."

"Tell me his name again."

"Lieutenant Cassada."

"Is that your name?"

"Yes, sir," Cassada said.

"Don't you know anything?" Dunning demanded and squeezed Cassada's shoulder as hard as he could, even grimacing as he did so.

In the November afternoon, deep blue, the clouds immaculate and tall, over the radio came a warning, first on tower frequency, then on that of each of the squadrons, repeated urgently, over and over,

"Attention, all 5th Group aircraft. Attention, all 5th Group aircraft. You are advised to return to base immediately. Return to base immediately."

Snow showers had been reported moving in from Luxembourg. The field was expected to go down to five hundred and one—five-hundred-foot ceiling and one-mile visibility—within twenty minutes.

Cassada was flying with Dumfries. They were at altitude about thirty miles out, the ground only occasionally visible through the solid, white clouds. They were in spread formation and Dumfries, who was leading, did not turn homeward but seemed to ignore the call.

"Green Lead, did you hear that?" Cassada said.

"Uh, negative. I couldn't read it. My radio is cutting in and out."

"They've ordered us to return to base. The weather's closing in."

"Roger," Dumfries said.

"They say it's going to five hundred and one within twenty minutes. Snow showers."

"Close it up, Two," Dumfries instructed.

Dumfries was completely without imagination, mechanical in his processes. Twenty minutes was to him an exact figure, a time when the ceiling would come down like the curtain in a theater. His nickname was Dum-dum, which he complained made no sense. "That's a kind of bullet," he said.

When Cassada joined up on his wing, Dumfries said, "Go Channel Eight, Green."

His own head went down as he looked to check that he had gone to the right channel, and almost at the same time he heard Cassada say, "Green Two."

"Roger."

They were at twenty-five thousand feet and began to let down. As they descended they could hear ships from the other squadrons entering traffic, calling on the break. From time to time the tower would block them out: "Attention, all 5th Group aircraft. Snow showers are reported north and west of the field, closing in. You are advised to return and land as soon as possible."

Cassada, hearing it—the calls, the other formations inbound—still new to it, felt a kind of electric happiness, a surge of excitement. Their speed was building. The air was heavier and more dense as they came down, nearing the cloud tops, then skimming them. He was confident they would get back to the field and at the same time felt a nervousness; it was in his arms and legs. The radio was alive with voices. From all directions planes were coming home.

As if following an actual path, Dumfries banked this way and that between the clouds and soon they were in the shadowy zone beneath, the brightness gone.

"Green has two at ten o'clock," Cassada called.

"I've got 'em."

Ahead the field appeared and like this, part of the instreaming pairs and flights of four, they entered traffic aware they were being observed like all the others, broke hard—some damp days it was possible to pull streamers, long, snake streaks of vapor pouring from the wingtips—came around and landed.

Though they had done nothing more remarkable than return without delay to the field, the repeated ominous warnings from the tower, the solid advancing wall of snow already visible, the many planes, some of them close behind, others breaking at the last minute overhead—all of it made for a feeling of achievement. It was as if they were returning from an actual mission, Cassada thought, a combat mission. He had missed all that, the thing that gave the major, the flight commanders, Isbell, even some of the pilots a greater authenticity. To return and land smoothly, in triumph.

Canopies open they taxied back towards the squadron at the other end of the field. There was a wood and wire fence to the side most of the way and beyond it the wide fields broken into clods and dark with manure. The smell in the air was the cold though. The first flakes of snow were already falling. The wind was from behind and warm waves of exhaust were blown forward together with the thin whistle of engines idling. Halfway along the fence, two drably dressed boys were standing motionless, hands in their pockets, their white faces plain to see, even the blotched red of their cheeks. Great as limousines the planes passed by them, bumping slightly on the expansion joints in the concrete. Tentatively, as if it might be ignored, one of the farmboys waved and Cassada, a god, arm resting on the cockpit railing, raised it and waved back. He was at last all he had dreamed of. The wave, he knew, had been recognition. Both boys were waving now, their arms jerking wildly. Dumfries had not seen them.

Cassada's parking spot was at the far end of the line. Dumfries waited at the edge of the ramp as he came trotting, his helmet still on to keep his ears warm. The snow was coming down harder. To the west it was white, earth and sky had vanished. It was a dry snow, small and hard, blowing along the ground like ashes, consuming the trees. The only place it was sticking was in the grass.

Joking, feeling good, they hung up their equipment and went into the briefing room, working the cold out of their faces.

"Wow," Cassada said, grinning.

"Good thing you heard that call, ordering us back."

"You wouldn't think it could go bad that quick. The weather."

Wickenden had walked in behind them carrying some letters he'd just received in his hand. He stood there, flicking the envelopes with his thumb.

"We just barely beat it in here, Captain," Cassada told him excitedly. "You could see the snow, big wall of it, right out to the west."

"I don't know about beating it in," Wickenden said, "but when you pulled out of here you blew stuff all over the place. You must have been using ninety percent."

"No, sir," Cassada said.

"Don't say, 'No, sir.' I was watching it. I saw a pair of chocks go flying twenty feet."

"No, sir," Cassada told him. "I don't know how much I used, but it wasn't over fifty or sixty. It wasn't even that."

"The hell it wasn't."

"It was fifty or sixty percent at most."

"Would you like to make that an official statement?"

"Official statement?"

"Yes. You know what that is? You can get court-martialed for making a false official statement."

"I'll make any kind of statement you want."

"Just watch what you're doing," Wickenden warned. He left the room.

Cassada looked down at his shoes. He kicked a little at something that wasn't there. Then, silent, his face expressionless, he began to take his flying gloves off, intent, pulling at the tip of each finger with his teeth to loosen the clinging leather.

"Well . . ." Dumfries began.

Cassada glanced at him.

"You'll get used to it," Dumfries said. "That's just the way he is."

Cassada said nothing. Finally he let out a sigh.

They stood near one of the radiators and talked about the flight, the earlier part of it. The snow was coming down more and more densely, curling as it neared the ground, sweeping along. Cassada was looking at it moodily, nodding every so often at something Dumfries said.

"Don't let it bother you," Dumfries advised toward the end.

"It isn't that," Cassada said after a moment. He slapped his gloves against his leg, staring blankly at the spot. "It's not just that. If he doesn't want to believe me, then don't ask me. It's the same as being called a liar. I'm not a liar."

"That's just the way he talks. It's different than in the other flights."

Dunning sat down in Isbell's office with a broad smile, laced his fingers across his stomach, and stretched out his legs. He had been looking at the flying time chart. "We got them this month, all right, Tommy," he said.

"Yes, sir. I think we do."

"Wait till Pine finds out."

It was the end of the month. They had outflown everyone, the yellowtails especially. "It would be nice to beat them for the year," Dunning added.

"If we get the maintenance."

Dunning nodded sagely as if he knew something about that.

"Well, Friday night," he said, gathering himself. "You getting up to the club before long?"

"I'll be there."

There were a few things left to be attended to and the last flight had yet to land. Isbell sat working at his desk. There was the faint sound of the adding machine in the outer office striking out sums in bursts. The operations clerks would be working late. He was looking out the window when there was a knock.

"Are you busy, Captain?" Cassada, slightly reticent, stood in the doorway. "I'd like to talk to you for a minute if I could."

"Sure. What's on your mind?"

"Is it all right if I close the door, sir?"

Isbell was still looking out the window. He turned his head. "What for?"

"It's something that I . . . it's something personal."

"It is, eh?" Isbell said unconcernedly.

He thought he heard them then and glanced out the window, then turned once more to Cassada who was wearing—Isbell was a little surprised by it—a look of impatience. "Sit down. What's the problem?"

"I wanted to ask about something. Maybe I should have come in sooner." He paused. "The thing is, ever since I've been in the squadron . . ."

"Which is what, all of three months?"

"Almost." Cassada began again: "When I started flying here it was with Lieutenant Grace and his flight."

Isbell felt a certain resentment rising in himself. "Yes. Grace had you for transition."

"I really learned a lot from him."

Cassada was looking down at his hands. "I wondered if there was a chance of my being put in his flight. I mean, if it wouldn't make too much difference. I think I'd pick up quite a bit from him."

"I'm sure you would."

Cassada looked up, uncertain at the tone. "To tell the truth I sort of expected—I suppose it was wrong because nobody had said anything to me one way or the other—to be in his flight from the beginning."

"Why?" Isbell said. He heard and saw them, coming along the

main taxiway, gliding like ghosts, like something borne on a river, through the fading light. The sound rose as they came closer, slowing.

"Well, because I'd flown with him all along."

The last ones were down. All was as it should be. Freed of concern then, fully attentive, "Just because I'm curious," Isbell said, "why did you wait until now to come in here?"

"I guess I shouldn't have."

"What is it, three or four weeks you've been in Captain Wickenden's flight now?"

"Yes, sir."

The last two planes were entering their hardstands, the crew chiefs skipping backwards as they came, waving them around in a tight, fetal turn, the engine cut even before the wheels came to a stop. The sound escaped, piercing and faint. It fell to nothing, to a deep, full silence.

"Well, what made you suddenly decide?" Isbell repeated. "There must be a reason."

Was it possible Isbell did not know what Wickenden was like, how overbearing, Cassada thought in confusion. Would he be angered to hear? "I guess I didn't have the nerve."

"The nerve?"

Cassada was silent.

"You can learn just as much about flying right where you are, if that's what you're really worried about. Maybe more."

"That's just it," Cassada insisted.

"What?"

"I think I'd do better. In fact I'm sure of it."

"Grace already has four men in his flight. If you were in it there'd be five and Wickenden would have three."

"I thought maybe there could be a switch. I might be able to get someone to agree to change."

"No," Isbell said instead of "Just try." "There's not going to be any change."

"Captain, I . . ."

Isbell made a gesture of what more do you want?

"Maybe I didn't explain it right."

"No, that's all. I have work to do."

A few minutes after Cassada had gone, Isbell picked up his cap and walked out of the office himself. There, inspecting the time chart with a grave air stood Wickenden, finishing a cigarette. "A lot of hours this month," he commented when Isbell was standing beside him.

"Yeah."

Some ashes had fallen to the floor near Wickenden's foot, Isbell saw. He'd been there for a while. It was hard to know for how long. "We'll be the top squadron this month," Isbell said, watching for a hint in Wickenden's face.

"Pine is probably holding back fifty hours till the last day."

"I know. He usually does. We figured that in."

"Ridiculous."

"Sure. It's a game."

"Next month we'll fall on our face."

"Next month is Tripoli."

"Oh, that's right."

"Coming to the club?"

Wickenden seemed still engrossed in the figures, the names of the pilots, how many hours each had flown, the total for each flight easily calculated. Isbell stared at the firm profile.

"I suppose I'm expected to," Wickenden said.

In the car he sat looking straight ahead, pointedly disaffected. How much he might have heard was hard to guess. Perhaps it was only his suspicions. He was slow to reveal himself, sometimes it took months. Sometimes he brought up things long past as if they had happened the day before. He began whistling through his teeth as they drove, difficult, touchy as an old dog. My ranking flight commander, Isbell thought wearily. The most experienced.

Some colonel up from Landstuhl had his 300SL parked below. They were admiring it from Harlan's room. They could see down into the rear window, the seats, tan leather and soft.

"They hand rub the lacquer between coats," Godchaux said.

It was after lunch. Harlan was picking his teeth.

"I like that color," Godchaux said.

"Maroon fades," Harlan said. Cars held no mystery for him. He had changed transmissions lying on his back in the hard dirt.

"There isn't a car that can touch it," Godchaux said.

"What does a car like that cost?"

"A lot."

"How much?"

"Six thousand dollars in Stuttgart. They guarantee you can do a hundred and fifty when you leave the factory."

"Where did you hear that?"

"It's a fact. Look at it. Look at the way it's humped over even standing still. They put the engine in there on an angle. It's canted.

It's not straight up and down. That's so they can keep the hood low."

"What's wrong with that Mercury you have?"

"It practically shakes to pieces at ninety."

"That's the roads over here," Harlan said.

"Even on the autobahn."

"Well, if I had six thousand dollars I wouldn't be buying that. I don't see the point of driving around in a year's pay."

"What a feeling, eh?"

"It looks fine, but what can you do in it that you can't do in yours?"

"A hundred and fifty," Godchaux said.

The sun had come out and was shining off the snow. The room bloomed with light.

"Looks like it's melting," Godchaux remarked. "Did you hear what Cassada said at lunch?"

"No, what?"

"He said he wanted to pack some up and send it home to his mother in a box."

Cassada had never seen snow.

"Oh, yeah? Where's he from? Alabama?"

"No, he's from Puerto Rico."

"Puerto Rico? You'd never know that from looking at him. Was he born there?"

"I think so. His father died or they got divorced. He lived with his mother."

"Puerto Rico," Harlan said. "Well, how'd he get in the American Air Force?"

"Puerto Rico's part of the United States."

"Since when?"

"I don't know. A long time."

"I must of missed hearing about it."

Harlan continued to pick his teeth. He had figured out Cassada. It was written all over him. He followed Grace through a couple of rolls on that first ride and got the idea he could fly. You could tell what he was thinking about just by looking in his eye, like a bull.

When Cassada was assigned to Wickenden's flight, Harlan had thought: perfect. Sometimes they show a little sense.

In with Wickenden and them was where he belonged. They could sit around when the ceiling went below a thousand feet and go over questions from the handbook. He'd fit in fine.

"What time is it?" Godchaux asked.

"Five to one."

"Come on, I'll give you a ride. We'd better be getting on back."

✝ ✝ ✝ ✝ ✝ ✝ ✝ ✝ ✝ ✝

The phone was ringing. From the bedroom Isbell called, "Can you get that? I'm busy."

"I'm sure it's for you," his wife said. She got up, keeping her place with a finger, and went over to the phone. "Marian Isbell." She had never learned and refused to say, "Captain Isbell's quarters."

It was Dunning.

"That husband of yours still up?" he asked.

"He's in the other room, Bud. Hold on."

"Listen," Dunning said, "don't bother getting him to come to the phone. Ask him if he'll pick me up in the morning."

"Who is it?" Isbell called.

"Bud Dunning." She had her hand over the mouthpiece. "Can you stop by for him in the morning?"

"Sure, what time?"

"What time, Bud?" she said, removing her hand.

"Oh, something like seven," Dunning said.

"Seven," Marian said to her husband.

"I'll be there," Isbell called.

"I heard him," Dunning said. "How are things going, Marian? Are you getting him all ready?"

"Oh, certainly."

"Well, that's good."

After Dunning hung up, she returned to her chair and began reading again. She could hear her husband moving about in the next room—the steps and pauses—packing. There was not a sound or a silence she could not identify, not only in her own apartment but in a hundred others. Feet were creaking on the ceiling. Water ran at certain times. There was the quiet at mealtimes, not to mention the smell of cooking, the familiar odors.

Isbell came into the hallway between the rooms. "Hey, honey, where are my socks?"

"They must be in the drawer."

"There's only four pairs in there."

"Don't shout, you'll wake them up. How many should there be?"

"I had lots of socks."

"Not so loud."

"It's just a normal tone of voice. I'm not going to go around whispering all the time. Where are the rest of them?"

"I don't know. In the wash, I guess."

"In the wash? You knew I was going to need them."

"Can't you buy some when you get down there?"

"Jesus, I must own twenty pairs already."

"All right. Just buy a few more. You can do that, can't you?"

"Sure. You know I have all the time in the world. I could probably even knit them if I have to. I just thought I'd take some of the ones I already have. That's one of the reasons I bought them."

"Not so loud. Please."

"They're not going to wake up."

"Well, you can try getting them back to sleep if they do."

After a pause Isbell said calmly, "Marian, you knew we were going a month ago."

"I forgot them," she said, "that's all. I didn't mean to. I just forgot."

Without saying anything more, Isbell turned away. After a while he brought two large bags, their side compartments bulging, into the hallway and set them down with a faint click of the metal studs on the bottom that helped them stand upright. Marian continued to read when he came into the living room.

"I set the alarm for six," he said. "If the weather's good we should be getting off first thing."

"It's supposed to be good, isn't it?" she said, still reading.

"The forecast is good."

"Six. Well, you'd better get to bed then. You'll need your sleep."

"What about you?"

"I think I'll finish this chapter," she said.

"How long is it?"

"Oh, I don't know." She held apart about thirty pages. "That much."

Isbell walked into the kitchen. There was the sound of ice being broken out of a tray. "You want a drink?" he called.

"Not really."

She knew the moment it started, what he would say and the way he would walk and act. It was the awful familiarity of it, of everything, the sound of him brushing his teeth and spitting in the sink, the moment when that stopped and light flooded the dark hall as he opened the bathroom door and with ominous weight lay down beside her. And afterwards when she lay awake looking out the window at other apartments, dark too, and seeing a bathroom light come on, just as they saw hers. They knew what was happening. She had asked him once not to turn it on.

"What's wrong?"

"People see it."

"Well, so what?"

"They know what's going on," she said feebly.

"No, they don't. That's absurd. How do they know? It could be the children. It might be anything."

"But it's not just anything."

Isbell came out with a drink and after a moment sat down and started to read a magazine. Marian found herself going over the same sentence two or three times. Her mind would not do what she wanted. She could hear him lazily turning the pages, moving in his chair, yawning.

"You sure you don't want a drink?"

"No, thanks."

"Come on."

"I don't feel like one."

He turned a few more pages.

"We're going to be down there for almost five weeks," he said.

"I know."

"That's more than a month."

She did not say what she felt which was, what difference does one time make? She simply didn't feel that way. It was a cold act, there was something selfish at the heart of it. Why was it that important? It wasn't; just some kind of male itch. But in the morning, she knew, he would be brief and irritable, even with all that lay ahead, Rome, crossing the Mediterranean, the islands, the North African shore. It would all be her fault. Why couldn't he just accept it, she thought? What did the other husbands do?

"It's getting late," Isbell finally remarked.

"I guess so."

"How much longer are you going to read?"

"Oh, a little while," she said.

"Come on."

"What do you mean?"

"You know what I mean. You can read all the time I'm gone. You've got five weeks."

"Just one more chapter," she said.

"What's wrong, Marian?"

"Nothing, really. I don't feel very well," she added.

"Stomach again?"

"I don't feel well, that's all."

He hated the whine in her voice. He went out on the balcony then. It was small, four or five paces long, and he stood there, leaning on the railing and looking out at the housing area. Lights were still on in many apartments. Only a few floors had dark stretches. The night was cold. The roads had ice on them and there was snow on the ground. The wind was whipping the shirt against his shoulder and back, but he stood as if not aware of it. The bitterness was warmth enough. On the floor below were Phipps and his wife, good-looking Carolina girl, nice legs. Every apartment had a wife in it, his included. You chose your wife yourself, that was the thing, but of course you didn't know what you were choosing. He had known after the first week, the deadness that lay between them, but he believed it might be overcome. He thought she would change through their being together, grow, reveal a hidden person, the one he had wanted and thought she might be. After five or ten minutes he went in to the bedroom and began undressing without a word.

# II

"WHERE'S CAPTAIN WICKENDEN?" DUNNING SAID.

† † † † † † † † † † †

"Where's Captain Wickenden?" Dunning said.

"Everyone's gone," Godchaux said. "We were the only two around. Harlan went out to mobile."

Dunning stood up. "How does it look to you out there?"

"Not too good."

Dunning suddenly turned his head and raised a hand. "Be quiet a minute," he said.

They looked at each other, waiting. The sound of the planes would grow from nothing. One moment, silence. The next, there it would be. Dunning's hand, however, came down.

"You hear anything?" he asked Godchaux.

"No, sir."

"Too soon, anyway. Where are they coming in from? Do you know?"

"There's no flight plan. Marseilles, I guess. We just heard them go over and called the tower to find out who it was." He looked towards the window. "I think they're going to have a little trouble."

"They can go to their alternate."

"I don't know. It's been down everywhere all day." He was a minister's son. Dunning remembered when he first reported in. Wonderful, the perfect background. Can he fly on Sundays, Isbell asked? They send you these people, Dunning had said, and expect you to make something out of them. Well, they had. "Is Harlan out there yet?" he asked.

Godchaux was at the window. "I can't see him from here," he said.

"Get on the other extension. Ask him what they're doing. Ask him what it looks like out there."

The phone rang then. It was the forecaster. He had altered his observation slightly—he'd added a broken layer at three hundred feet. Dunning asked for the weather at the nearest alternates, everything within a hundred miles, and as the forecaster read them off, he scribbled them down, half-listening for the planes. Finally he stopped writing. The reports were worse and worse, the weather was no better anywhere.

"The only alternate open in Europe right now is Marseilles," the forecaster said.

"What about England?"

"One moment, Major," the forecaster said, his voice becoming distant as he reached for a clipboard. "I have my doubts."

Godchaux, on the phone to mobile, could hear the radio out there. He put a hand over his receiver. "They're on final again, Major," he said.

"How far out? Give it here," Dunning said, reaching. His look of self-possession was gone. In its place was nothing, the face of an officer who might still possibly be on the list to be promoted.

Just as Godchaux passed the phone they heard them, the sound low at first and then expanding, opening up, seeming to head for and almost pass over them. Dunning at the window knew what it meant. They were not landing. They had missed again and were going by, everything hanging, heavy and nose-high like a pair of sick men in the grey evening, the noise even louder when they had passed barely below the clouds, slipping in and out of them, the red tails visible, then into the clouds again and gone. The voice of the forecaster, now incidental and remote, came over the phone, ". . . down everywhere in England. I don't see anything open. Major?"

At the same time there was the controller's voice over the radio in mobile, "Fortify White, turn to three six zero . . ."

"Harlan!" Dunning said on the phone. "Hello!"

"Climb to twenty-five hundred feet," the controller was directing.

"Harlan! Mobile control!"

There was the sound of the phone being picked up.

"Yeah, what is it, Billy? They screwed up another one."

"This is Major Dunning."

"Oh, sorry, Major. They just missed another approach. Maybe you better come out here."

"I'm coming right out," Dunning said. "What about the weather? How does it look out there?"

"You better come out, Major."

"I'll be right there."

Godchaux was pointing to the other receiver from which the forecaster's voice still came tinnily. "What about him?"

"Oh, hang up. Let's go."

The operations vehicle, a khaki-colored van, was parked outside. The engine started immediately. Dunning, in the driver's seat, seemed huge. He struggled with the gearshift, shoving it one way then the other.

"Push down on it, Major. You have to push down on it."

They lurched backwards. Dunning stamped on the brake and the van heaved to a stop. They started forward again, down the taxiway, picking up speed.

"Which way are you going?" Godchaux called.

"Right across."

"It's pretty rough out there."

"Hold on!"

Dunning was looking towards each end of the runway as they drove, half expecting the planes to appear from anywhere. Towards the far end the clouds seemed a little higher. That might be it, to bring them in downwind, but as he looked he saw that it was shifting all the time, spaces were revealed and then covered over again.

At the intersection Dunning didn't turn but went straight ahead, off the taxiway, jolting across the uneven ground, still watching for the planes. There was a sudden slam as he drove into a hollow, the van shot up and hit again on the front wheels. Godchaux was holding on to the seat. Dunning had the accelerator to the floor. Ahead was the mobile control with the shadow of Harlan showing through the flat glass. He opened the door as they came running towards him. Dunning pushed past and into the narrow space between the two counters on which were binoculars, frayed magazines, and a flare pistol. The radio hummed beneath.

"Where are they?" he asked.

"They're on the downwind."

"Have they said how much fuel they have?"

"I'm not sure. About a thousand pounds, I think."

Dunning felt a moment of relief, not at the number but at having made it out in time, like someone who finds a piece of wreckage to cling to in a stormy sea. He looked to the north as he waited for the voices. All was calm. The sky was the cold grey of lead. It touched the hills. Three birds were standing in the middle of the empty runway, almost on the white center line. There were about twenty more minutes of daylight. The beacon had become brighter. It was skimming the base of the clouds, increasing in contrast each time around. No, he was imagining that. All was quiet, closed until morning, when the voice of the controller who was in a yellow and white checkered van at the far end of the field came up clear,

"Fortify White, turn left to one five zero and descend to two thousand feet for base leg."

Godchaux, crowding in beside them, pulled the door closed behind him.

"Leave it open," Dunning ordered. "I want to hear them if I can."

"Perform final cockpit check," the controller said. "Gear should be down and locked. Final flap setting at pilot's discretion."

After a moment or two came the reply,

"White has gear down and locked."

It was a hurried voice, a little nervous and high. Dunning tried to think; they were his planes, Fortify, but the voice . . .

"That's not Isbell," he said. He turned to Harlan. "That isn't him."

"No, sir."

"What's wrong? Why isn't he leading?"

"His radio's out," Harlan said.

His radio was out. He wasn't leading. The wingman was leading. In an instant everything had changed.

On the flight line in Tripoli forty or fifty planes were parked in a long, glinting row. Behind them where the blacktop ended the ground dropped away to a broad depression where seawater was evaporated in great, shallow beds. The first rule of gunnery camp was always the same, "Don't piss in the Salt Flats." Facing the planes was a line of corrugated iron huts with an occasional tent or some canvas rigged on poles to provide shade. The ground crews, many of them stripped to the waist, were squatting under the wings with wrenches, dropping the external tanks. Two of the three squadrons had landed. The first yellowtails were just taxiing in. The 72nd. Another flight of them was on the break. Pilots sat on their gear in the afternoon sun, waiting for the bus to take them to their tent area.

All of it echoed the war that had been fought here, not so many years earlier, along the narrow band of desert near the sea. The same brown tents, the sun, the dust, the overriding focus. In all likelihood the same bus, a tilting wreck with an Arab driver and no fixed schedule. Usually it would leave just when someone was coming to board or running towards it. The driver, a hand on the door lever, would start the engine in no apparent hurry and, as if unable to hear the shouts, swing the door shut and drive off. Twenty minutes later, sometimes more, at the far end of the parking area, white dust rising behind, the bus would return, the brakes squealing as it slowly came to a stop.

Struggling with their bags, pilots climbed aboard and lurched down the aisle. In the back, Grace sat down near Wickenden.

"Five dollars a man, what do you say?"

Wickenden shook his head.

"Five dollars, the same as last time. That's fair enough."

Wickenden only smiled a little, like a man reading a book.

"How about it?" Grace said. "That's reasonable. What's wrong? Don't you think you can outshoot us?"

Harlan, grinning, turned in his seat. Wickenden looked out the window.

"Don't you have any confidence in your boys?"

"I have confidence in them," Wickenden said. "More than I have in yours."

"OK then."

"I also have a new man who's never fired before."

"Who? Cassada?" He had not flown a plane down. He was coming, with several others, in a transport. "Hell, he'll probably make expert," Grace said.

"I'm sure."

The bus was full. "Hey, driver," they were beginning to call, "let's go!"

"I'm just as bad off," Grace said. "I've got Fergy."

"He's an experienced man," Wickenden countered wearily.

"You're damned right!" Ferguson called out.

"You know yourself," Grace went on, ignoring this, "that it's usually two weeks before he can even find the tow ship much less get hits."

"That was *one* day when the visibility was lousy!" Ferguson called.

"Driver! Let's go!" they were shouting.

The driver sat with his hands in his lap. He was wearing the jacket from a blue suit, chalky and worn. It looked as if he'd been carrying bags of flour. He sat staring ahead as if that were his only duty.

"Then it's another two weeks before you can get him to come in any closer than fifteen hundred feet," Grace went on. "You know that." He had a white spot of bone in his nose that gleamed when he smiled.

"Driver! Let's go!"

"You're no worse off than I am," Grace said.

Wickenden's mouth was set in a line.

"Everybody else is willing. Reeves is, I know."

Silence.

"How about it?"

Instead of answering, Wickenden raised his hands to his mouth and in a surprisingly powerful voice commanded, "Let's get going, driver!"

As if in response the driver bent forward and lazily turned the ignition key. The engine started. With a jolt the bus began to move.

Grace had given up. Most of it had only been for show; he knew Wickenden wouldn't gamble—too humiliating if he lost. Wickenden liked to read military history. He could explain that the essence of generalship was to fight only when you were thoroughly prepared and certain you could win. Maybe that was what they taught them up there, Grace thought. It certainly wasn't like the ROTC.

These were the days, the airplanes clean—without external tanks—at their fastest and most maneuverable, the maintenance hardworking, weather flawless, the competition intense. In North Africa it was gunnery and only gunnery. The first tow ship took off early at eight, climbing at a steep angle with the target, a long, fabric panel, trailing behind. A few minutes later the first flight of firing ships, trim as hornets, followed.

Isbell was leading. The three others were in string, behind. They hadn't spotted the tow ship yet. Finally they found it crossing the shoreline, insect small, and circled above watching it over the dark water, slow, deliberate, like a ship sailing to Malta with, instead of wake, the dash of white behind.

The sun was always bad early in the day, naked and low, the reflections drifting across the windshield glass. Sometimes they blanked out the target, even the tow ship, in sky that had a soft blue cast to it, the light pale and lacking contrast. But it was smooth then. The air was still. Not a tremor.

Banking from side to side, hand held up to block the sun, Isbell kept the tow ship in sight. The familiar excitement mounting within, he watched it reach altitude and roll out on course.

"Red Tow on station, on course."

"We have you in sight, Red."

"Roger. You're cleared in to fire."

Isbell led them alongside, several thousand feet above.

"Lead in," he called and started down towards the strip of white, an inch long it seemed.

The tow ship was at twenty thousand feet, ten or fifteen miles from shore, red desert to the south, hard blue sea below. There was a full, damp quality to the air. Long streamers curved through it marking one's path. All unhurried, all unalterable. There was a rhythm, mostly of pauses but regular, like section hands driving a spike.

"Two in," Phipps called.

Isbell had reversed his turn and was coming in from the rear of the target which shone in the light like a grail. His gunsight had locked on. His speed was increasing. He quickly checked it, three forty. He could feel the G's as he held the turn and then, in a rush, the climax when he was in range for a second or two with the target suddenly expanding in size until the final instant when he broke off.

"Lead off," he called.

"Three in," he heard and as he was climbing back up, "Two off."

He had not fired on the initial pass, but on the five following ones, all just so, not a single bad one, bursts of about a second, long and even. He was getting hits, he was sure of it. It felt exactly right. The ship seemed firm under his hand, obedient to the last moment, the white rectangle slowly enlarging, not much at first then faster and faster like an express going by. The bullets left traces of smoke as they vanished into the cloth.

If the sight was any good, that was the only thing. When the aircraft were listed he had given Cassada his choice, then Phipps, then Harlan. He had taken the one that was left.

"I have a feeling I'm going to hit today," Cassada had said.

"Glad to hear it."

"I just have the feeling."

On the way back, as they were joining up, Isbell asked, "Red Four? How'd you do?"

"I got hits," Cassada said confidently.

They came in over the bay, the boats at anchor beneath them, the buoys, and turned just short of the city, white in the early day, to line up with the runway five miles off. Isbell looked to the side. They were in echelon, one motionless canopy beyond the other.

"Red Lead," he called as he whipped to the side, "on the break."

After debriefing they stood around and waited for the tow ship to come back. Harlan had picked up some pebbles and was shaking them in his fist.

"How'd you do?" Isbell asked.

Harlan shrugged. "All right, I guess."

"What color were you firing?"

The heads of the bullets were dipped in paint to identify who had fired them.

"Blue," Harlan said.

"Yellow," Cassada murmured, almost to himself, as if to cards or dice.

Along the far side of the runway, the tow ship came in sight, flying low, ready to drop.

"What color did you say?" Isbell asked.

"Yellow," Cassada repeated.

A truck came from the direction of the runway, the dust rising. It pulled up and the bundled target was thrown off. It was unrolled and hung lengthwise on the scoring board. Isbell was at the tail end hooking the nails through. The end was slightly frayed but it was still almost full length, twenty-eight feet. They stood with the first look at it. There were red and blue spread through it and one burst of green in front near the bar, but no yellow.

"Damn it," Cassada said in disbelief. "Where's the yellow?"

Finally Harlan found one at the very bottom near the edge.

"Here you are," he said.

Cassada stood helplessly. It was as if he had lost the power to move.

"Here you are, dead-eye," Harlan said. "You're right. You did hit it."

Cassada looked at the single hole. He seemed dazed. He took the fabric in his hand.

"I can't understand it," he said.

"You had a good airplane," Isbell said. "You were probably firing out of range."

Cassada shook his head.

"How do you know?"

"No, sir. I was in there."

"Well, you were doing something wrong."

"I can't understand it. I did everything right. I had the right air-speed, the G's. The pipper was right on."

"We'll have to look at your film."

"I forgot. It's still out in the airplane."

"You'd better go get it before it gets lost."

Looking at the ground, carrying all the disappointment he could bear, Cassada walked towards the ramp. Phipps had picked up the clipboard and was marking down the hits as Harlan called them out. Blue. Red. Blue. Three reds. Blue. When they had finished, Isbell had forty-six and Harlan forty. A crowd had gathered around to watch the scoring. It was the best target thus far.

"Damn fine shooting," Wickenden commented.

Dunning strolled up with a cup of coffee in his hand. They were unhooking the target.

"Just a minute, gentlemen, just a minute. Let it hang up there for a while. Give these other squadrons a chance to look at it."

He picked up the score sheets. He was reading them when Cassada came back. Dunning did not look up.

"Were you firing on this one, Lieutenant?" he asked blandly.

"Yes, sir."

"What color?"

"Yellow."

"I don't see too many yellow hits here," Dunning said, pursing his mouth speculatively. "What seemed to be the trouble, bad sight?"

"No, sir," Cassada said. "The sight was good."

Dunning waited.

"Major, I don't understand it," Cassada admitted.

Dunning made a slight sound of acknowledgement.

"Oh, let's face it," Harlan muttered. "You're not about to hit anything."

Cassada looked at him, unable to speak. The words were jammed in his throat.

"What did you get?" he said. His cheekbones were burning.

"I don't know," Harlan shrugged. "Forty-eight percent. Something like that."

Cassada stood there, humiliation coloring his fairness.

"Good enough for you?" Harlan said. He was dropping the pebbles from one hand to the other.

"I'll beat it," Cassada said.

Dunning was watching with a cool, remote smile.

"You will, eh?" Harlan said.

"Yes, I'll beat it."

"You'll be lucky if you even qualify."

Cassada's hands were trembling. He had put them in his pockets.

"I'll beat any score you make," he said.

"Just put up your money."

Cassada stood there. He tried to think for a moment of what he was doing. Harlan was pouring the pebbles from hand to hand. That was the only sound. The vehicles passing, the aircraft engines being started, all of it seemed far off.

"Well?"

"All right," Isbell broke in. He was about to say, that's enough, but Dunning lifted a hand in restraint.

"Look . . ." Isbell nevertheless began.

"Captain Isbell," Dunning warned.

"I'll bet," Cassada said. "How much?"

"Just whatever you want," Harlan said.

"Fifty dollars."

Isbell was shaking his head in disgust.

"Hell. Is that all?" Harlan said.

"I'll bet whatever you want to bet. A month's pay. Is that good?"

"Yours or mine?"

"I don't care. Yours," Cassada said.

Harlan sniffed calmly. He dropped the pebbles he was holding to the ground. "All right, that's a bet." He held out a hand.

Cassada ignored it. "My word's enough," he said.

"Your word, hell. Shake on it."

Cassada didn't move. "You have enough witnesses," he said.

He stayed at the target afterwards, alone, staring at it as one might at some construction where everything had gone wrong. Isbell went back into the operations hut. Wickenden followed him.

"That's about what I would expect of him," Wickenden said. "Didn't surprise me at all. He's a fool."

"Somebody should have stopped them. I wanted to," Isbell said.

"What for?" Wickenden said. "That's the only way someone like that ever learns."

In Sunday quiet, in the creaking of canvas, Wickenden lay on his cot reading. When he turned a page he folded it back, doubled, so he could hold the book in one hand. With the other he brushed at his arm or leg from time to time, at an annoying fly. Dumfries sat writing a letter. From the next tent a voice occasionally drifted over, a voice that was confiding to Grace, confessing to him. He *had* to hit—something like that—it was hard to make out the exact words. In any case, Wickenden ignored them and the slight they represented. He read on.

Idle Sundays. Dunning was off playing golf with the group commander and group ops on a course that was mostly sand dunes. Godchaux and Phipps had driven the silken black road that ran along the coast—the same road on which the guns and sun-baked armor of the Afrika Korps and British Eighth Army had fought back and forth—to one of the ruins, Leptis Magna, with its chalk-white columns and vacant amphitheater scorched by the sun, a great tumbled quarry near the sea. He and Phipps wandered the wide avenues. The Romans had built three cities along the coast, Phipps explained. "Tripoli, three cities. That's what it means."

"Is that right? Where'd you find that out?"

"Sabratha is the other one."

"Why'd they build this? What did they do here?"

"This was a big city. Everything."

"Let's go this way," Godchaux said. He had seen a man and two girls walking along a nearby street of what, ages past, had been shops.

They turned out to be Italian and stopped for a moment. One of the girls, dark-haired, was wearing a tight top, a sailor's shirt. She stood with the sunlight gleaming on her while Godchaux tried to make conversation, but none of the three spoke English.

"You know any Italian?" Godchaux turned to Phipps.

"Cunati does."

"That's not going to help us. So, listen," he said to the Italians, "you live here, in Tripoli?"

They didn't understand, however, and wandered off. Godchaux watched them. The shirt was above white pants, also tight. "Jesus Christ," he said.

"Let's go down to the harbor," Phipps said.

"Yeah. You can throw me in."

"What for?"

"Take a cold shower. That's what they used to say."

"The girl?"

"Jesus."

They wandered on. The sea was strewn with brown sea grass. They didn't catch sight of the trio again.

Harlan and Ferguson were in town at the Del Mahari, sitting among the short dark men in business suits and the heavy-looking women. Cassada had been over talking to Grace about gunnery again, Ferguson commented.

"Oh, yeah?"

"He's really focused on it."

"Is that right? Well, he can talk all he wants." Harlan was reading the menu. "The bird that talks the most is the parrot," he added, "and *it* can't fly."

"*Teniente?*" the waiter asked.

"I'll take the sirloin, rare. *Capisce?* Rare."

"I'll have the same thing," Ferguson said. He was wearing sunglasses. His blond hair looked dirty. He was the same size as Harlan but more amiable. Everyone liked him.

Grace hadn't been able to tell Cassada much. It would have been disloyal to Harlan, to a member of his flight. He just went over the usual things. Make sure the ball is in the center, you don't want to be even the slightest bit uncoordinated. Try and shoot at a low angle off. The best scores have hits nearly as long as your little finger. Hits the size of your fingernail are no good.

Day after day. Gradually the men on the line became darkened by the sun, and the pilots, too, their hands and faces. Officers and men grew together here, more than anywhere else. They pitched in. They knew one another's names. The men had their champions, the pilots their favorite crew chiefs and armorers.

Abrams, the operations clerk, worked long hours, as well. He was short and overweight with red cheeks. Isbell was not his favorite nor was he Isbell's. Too many mistakes, Isbell said. He went over the figures, the gunnery reports.

"What are seven and sixteen?" he said.

"Where is that, sir?"

"Right here."

"Seven and sixteen," Abrams said. "Twenty-three."

"You've got twenty-two."

Abrams looked at the sheet.

"I don't know what happened there," he said.

"It's a mistake is what happened."

"I'll fix it," Abrams said. He knew Isbell wanted to humiliate him. The figures were not that important anyway. Who would find out they had fired three thousand and eighteen rounds instead of three thousand and seventeen? Who would care? There were mountains of ammunition out there. They could lose track of a whole case of it in supply, no one would bat an eye, but let it be just one bullet off. . . . In the other squadrons it was nothing like this. That was his luck, to be in this one.

The projector in the film room—a plywood booth with a blanket over the entrance to make it dark—was running. From time to time it would stop, go into strained reverse, then start forward again. The two of them were in there; Abrams could hear their voices plainly in the empty building.

"You wasted rounds on every one of those passes. You started to break off before you were finished firing. You have to follow through, just like everything else. Let up on the trigger, track for a split second, *then* break off"

"Let's run it through again."

"No, that's enough. It's hard on the eyes."

Lifting a corner of the blanket, Isbell came out rubbing his eyes with the heels of his hands. He waited until Cassada rewound the reel and put it away.

"I'll tell you something else," he said when Cassada emerged. "You're pressing in a little too close. You're going to fly right into the target one of these times. That target bar is made of iron. Start breaking off at six hundred feet like you're supposed to."

"I'm not going to run into it, Captain."

"Listen to me. You'll have a major accident on your hands and the major and I will get the blame. Break off at six hundred feet."

"Yes, sir."

"Go ahead and catch the bus. I'm going to be here for a while."

"What does the schedule look like for tomorrow? I need missions."

"You'll see it. Go on, now."

Cassada hesitated at the door as if he were going to say something, then let go of the jamb and walked out, heading towards the bus stop.

Isbell turned to Abrams,

"All finished?" he asked.

"I'm just checking it over."

"That doesn't sound like you."

Abrams lowered his head as if in even greater effort. "Sir," he said, "I always check it."

"You do?"

"Yes, sir."

"It's a good thing we're not running a bank," Isbell said. "Here, give it to me."

He took the page and scribbled his name at the bottom of it without looking at the figures. "How many mistakes are in there?" he asked, handing it back.

"Captain, it's correct. I checked it. There are no mistakes."

"That would set a record," Isbell said.

He began reading the score sheets on the wall. They had been posted at the end of the day.

"Those are up to the minute," Abrams offered.

There was no reply. He began to type the envelope the reports went into.

"We're not doing too bad," Isbell murmured, almost to himself.

"No, sir. We're ahead of the other squadrons. I keep tabs."

"I know."

Abrams shook out the black typewriter cover and began to put it back on. Through the window he could see the lone figure, waiting.

"Do you think the lieutenant will win the bet?" he asked.

"I doubt it," Isbell said. "What do the men think?"

"Well . . . they're betting on Lieutenant Harlan, I guess."

"Probably a good idea," Isbell said. "Who are you betting on?"

"Oh, I haven't made any bets. Lieutenant Cassada is certainly trying though, isn't he?"

"Yeah, he's trying."

Abrams glanced out the open window again. "He sort of puts me in mind of the turtle."

Cassada was walking slowly back and forth, a few steps each way, watching for the bus.

"Which turtle?"

"You know, Captain. The one that beat the rabbit. In the story."

"That's a little lesson for you, isn't it?"

"He might come from behind, like the turtle."

"We'll see. It's a good thing he believes in himself."

"Yes, sir."

"Doesn't always mean a lot. I can tell you that from experience."

In flying school Cassada had been an enthusiastic student. He loved flying and had never, from the very first, felt any fear. When he received his wings he could not repress his excitement and pride. He'd had two years of college and for a while the love, somewhat dramatic, of a girl in Savannah who wanted to be an actress, but all that did not matter compared to what lay ahead. He was going to join the ranks, go to a squadron overseas. He was going to make a name for himself, become known.

Somehow it had not happened. He had found himself under the command of an unsympathetic officer who neither liked nor tried to understand him. He had never imagined this as a possibility. It had stolen all the joy out of life. The squadron was like a large family with a history he was not really part of, and he felt like a foster child in the house of a stern father. He looked forward only to the day that Wickenden would be gone. He disliked Wickenden and could hardly look at him. He would receive a bad effectiveness report from him, he knew, and already accepting that, he behaved with indifference, almost sullenly and ready to take offense at the least provocation.

Challenging Harlan, a veteran in a flight he would have liked to belong to, was an impulsive act of pride and defiance, though he secretly believed he might win them by it and, outdoing Harlan, show he was worthy to belong. If only he could even come close!

He'd had no success. The many things that had to be done correctly, he could not seem to put together. The secret eluded him. He had gone several times to the bore-sighting pit where the planes, mounted on large jacks, had their guns adjusted and then fired, a round at a time, to be sure they converged at the right point. He had kept a list of which airplanes made good scores. The armament men knew him and were fond of him, but try as he might he could not do better than twelve or fifteen percent until one morning when suddenly, as if a key had been turned, everything had come together. The air had been smooth, the passes good, and even time itself seemed to have slowed a little so that the target, leaning slightly, large and white, the tail of it fluttering, had been there for a fraction of a second longer than usual, and he came down to find it filled with green hits, the color he had been firing! He'd gotten thirty-two percent, more than double anything he'd achieved before. He could hardly believe it, but there it was, green holes all through it, thirty-two percent! His spirits soared. He would do even better.

"Looks like you finally got the idea," Isbell told him.

"Not bad," Phipps said. "What did you do, close your eyes?"

"I just did what they tell you to do."

"Oh yeah, what's that?"

He didn't reply. It had been early, the first mission of the day, the others hadn't come down to the line after breakfast yet, but they would. They would see the target hanging there. The word would spread. He was elated, filled with fresh energy.

"You firing green?" Wickenden asked.

"Yes, sir."

Wickenden nodded. Not even a word of approval. It hardly mattered. Cassada was smiling to himself. He felt like dancing. There were nine days of gunnery to go.

In the tent area they had a five-gallon container filled with ice, grapefruit juice, and vodka on a table in the sun. The closing party. Pilots in dirty flying suits. The heat of the day.

"Hey, Wes," Isbell called. "Have a drink."

"No, thanks, Captain," Harlan said.

"Join the fun."

"I can have enough fun just watching everybody make a fool of themselves."

"Come on." Isbell was unsteady on his feet.

"No, thanks."

"Ah, you're missing the best part."

"I don't know about that," Harlan said.

"That's what we come down here for. To eat soup together."

"Soup?"

"That's right. Eat soup and drink screwdrivers."

Gunnery was over. The pickup carrying the target had come in after the last flight and as it slowed the airman in the passenger seat had given a thumbs-up sign, many hits. A crowd watched as it was being unfolded. Near the front end was a great scattering of red. Cassada. Mixed in was blue which was what Phipps had been firing. In the middle of the target, relative emptiness. Harlan stood with the onlookers. His highest score had been a forty percent accomplished during the first weeks and his overall average was impressive, in the low thirties. Dunning had only one score out of the twenties because he insisted on flying his own aircraft which was not a good gunnery ship as the rest of them knew. They would moan when scheduled to fly it.

Isbell was counting the holes. "Red. Red. Two reds. Blue," he called out. "Another blue. Red. Two more blues."

Cassada was almost holding his breath, hoping madly. It was the final mission and his last chance. There were not many reds in the middle but at the tail end of the target was a great, redeeming burst.

Dunning came up puffing on a cigar and with his shirt off. Immense and white-skinned, to Harlan he confided, "You might be having a little trouble, Lieutenant."

"No trouble, Major," Harlan said as if he were sure.

"He said he'd outshoot you."

"We'll see. He hasn't come close yet."

He could hear the annoying hits being called out, blue, red, red, three reds . . .

"I don't know now," the major said.

Harlan said nothing, waiting. He was not watching Isbell or Cassada, he was looking at the tail of the target. The light made it hard to see from where he stood.

"Lot of red there," Dunning said. He seemed to be enjoying it. Harlan was counting to himself. It looked to be a high score, one that could go down to the last hole.

There was a crowd around as Isbell added. It was not quite forty. It was thirty-six percent.

At the party, Cassada came around the side of one of the tents, his sleeves rolled up and the cup of his mess kit almost full. Browned and slender, hair paled by the sun, he looked like a veteran. He found Grace and some others standing in a group. Harlan was among them, his back turned. Cassada walked up to them. He looked at Harlan.

"I guess I owe you some money," he said.

It was as if Harlan didn't hear.

"I don't have all of it, I just have part of it now."

Harlan turned. Very deliberately he said, "The bet was for a month's pay."

"I'll have to give you the rest later."

"You were ready to bet but you can't back it up?"

"Take this. I'll give you the rest after payday." He held out a check. Harlan made no move to accept it. Cassada tried to put it in Harlan's hand but Harlan made no attempt to take it. The check fell to the ground. The others were watching.

"You don't have the money." Harlan said. "I could of guessed it."

"There it is."

"Where? I don't see it."

"It's right there," Cassada said. "Better pick it up. It's the only time I'm going to be paying."

"What's all that about next payday, then?"

"That's the other part."

"I don't want parts. Where's the money?"

Cassada, face burning, pushed the oblong piece of paper towards Harlan with his foot. There was a terrible silence.

"Hell, Wes," Grace said, "go on and take it."

Harlan's broad face filled with scorn and also defiance.

"Why don't you just say, I don't have it, buddy?" Harlan said to Cassada. "I just don't have it."

Phipps, who was watching, bent down and picked up the check.

He passed it to Harlan. "Why don't you guys act like grown-ups?"

Harlan took the check, folded it, took out his wallet and put it inside. Godchaux had his arm around him.

"Don't hide it away. Aren't you going to buy everyone drinks at the club?"

"I don't think anybody needs more drinks."

"Come on," Godchaux said.

"Go ahead and win your own money."

"I think we ought to have a pool next time," Grace said, "and the top three split it. Half to the high scorer and on down."

"All right with me," Harlan said.

"If we could get 'A' Flight to join in we'd clean up," Grace said. "I see myself getting first place, then maybe Godchaux, then you."

"I'm third?" Harlan said.

"I'd put you first except for one thing."

"What's that?"

"You don't drink," Grace said, seemingly serious.

"Shit."

Near the showers a wrestling match had broken out and they were calling for Dunning, who was in his tent, to come and show how he had played end at Auburn. The party was becoming disorderly and also spreading past the tents to other squadrons having parties of their own.

Sometime after dark Dumfries came into the tent and turned on the light. Cassada was lying on his cot. Dumfries thought at first he was asleep, but he had merely closed his eyes against the light.

"I didn't know anyone was in here," Dumfries said. "Aren't you going over to the club?"

"No."

"I'm not either. I only had one cup of that stuff. I think it was doggone strong. Some of them are really drunk. Did you have a lot?"

"No."

"I don't know what-all was in it."

Cassada rolled over onto his side and closed his eyes. "Why don't you turn off that light?" he said.

"I just want to get undressed," Dumfries said. He sat down on his footlocker and began to unlace his boots. "You still have your shoes on."

"I know."

There was noise from the major's tent and from between the tents, shouting and singing. Dumfries had taken off one boot. He was talking about big fraternity parties he remembered although that was all beer, he said. Mostly beer. Cassada seemed not to be listening.

"Gee, it was too bad to lose that bet," Dumfries said.

Cassada's thoughts seemed elsewhere.

"I used to bet a lot myself," Dumfries said, "at school. Mostly on football games, the World Series, things like that. After a while I really had a reputation, as a matter of fact. You probably wouldn't believe it, the way I am now. They used to call me Little John. After John Cuneo. Of course, it was only kidding. He's a real big gambler over in Sacramento. Maybe you've heard of him, John Cuneo.

"But then I used to win so much it wasn't fun anymore, and I promised my mother I'd stop. She used to say, where'd you get all that money from? She never liked it very much. You know how they are. Aren't you going to take off your shoes?"

Cassada rolled over and shook his head as if in bewilderment. "I don't know what I'm doing here," he muttered.

"What'd you say?"

"I don't know. Turn out the light."

Dumfries had taken off his other boot. He was still talking about his mother. Something went past him. It was a shower clog. "Hey!" he said. A shoe flew by and out the tent entry. Then another clog.

"Hey, what do you think you're doing?" Cassada was sitting up, throwing. The bulb exploded.

"What was that for?" said Dumfries in the darkness.

"Turning out the light," Cassada said, settling back.

"You got glass all over the place," Dumfries complained. "Someone's going to cut their feet. Wait until Captain Wickenden comes in. He's going to be mad."

"He won't know the difference," Cassada said.

"Well, I've got to walk over it in the dark. I don't want to walk on a lot of glass."

Cassada did not reply. Stepping with care, Dumfries left the tent and went towards the showers to get a bulb from over one of the sinks. When he got back, Cassada was gone. Dumfries took the broom and swept the glass into a pile near the entrance. He was looking carefully to see if he'd gotten all of it.

"What are you doing?" Wickenden asked.

"Oh. Just sweeping up some glass. Cassada broke the bulb."

"How'd that happen?"

"He threw a shoe at it."

"Why didn't he sweep it up?"

"Gee, Captain, I don't know. He would have just left it lying there."

"Bring that broom over here. You missed some."

"Yes, sir."

Wickenden went over to his cot. "If I cut my foot," he said, "he's going to sweep this tent with his toothbrush."

"Yes, sir."

"I'm not kidding."

There was going to be trouble, Dumfries thought.

# III

Godchaux had stepped outside . . .

Godchaux had stepped outside and was facing the direction they would be coming from. The light had faded, the last, deceiving light. A thousand pounds, Dunning was saying to himself, a thousand pounds, fifteen minutes, with Isbell hanging there not able to do a thing. If it was Godchaux with him it would be different, but it was never someone like Godchaux.

"Turn left to zero six zero," the controller said. "Maintain two thousand feet."

"Zero six zero."

"Roger, White. Now stand by on this channel for your final controller."

Almost immediately another voice broke in.

"Fortify White, this is your final controller. How do you read?"

There was no answer.

"Fortify White, this is final controller. How do you read me?"

Silence. Dunning had the mike in his hand and was about to call himself when finally there came, replying as if just now part of it all,

"Fortify White."

"How do you read me?"

"Five square."

"Roger," the controller said, adding with calmness, "the tower advises that the field has now gone below minimums."

Of course it has, Dunning thought. Goddamn it, I knew it when I first called. Look out the window, I said, look out the goddamn window!

"You're advised to proceed to your alternate. Call outbound over the beacon at thirty-five hundred feet."

"Negative," Dunning interrupted. "Bring them in here!"

"The field is closed, White."

"This isn't White. This is mobile control."

"Roger. Stand by one," the controller said.

"Stand by nothing! This is Major Dunning in mobile. Bring them in. Bring them in here!"

There was the end of another transmission that had been blocked out,

". . . an emergency!"

"What'd you say, White?"

"You were blocked, White," the controller said. "Say again."

"I'm declaring an emergency! I'm declaring an emergency!"

"Roger," the controller said. In the background the intercom from the tower could be heard. "Can you proceed to Landstuhl?" the controller asked.

"Negative. I'm down to nine hundred pounds. I can't divert."

Finally, after agonizing moments, the controller said, "Roger." And as if it were ordinary routine, "Your position is six miles out on final. Correct two degrees left to zero five eight. Make that zero five five, drifting slightly to the right of on-course."

"Zero five five."

"Your gear should be down and locked. Uh, do you request crash equipment to stand by?"

"That's affirmative."

"Roger. We're notifying the tower." There was a pause. "Five and one half miles. At this time you need not reply to any further transmissions. Correct further left to zero five three. Zero five three is your new heading, bringing you slowly back to the on-course. Zero five three."

The only sound was this almost self-involved voice. Five miles. Back right to zero five five. The waiting was interminable. Zero five five. Coming up to glide path.

The three of them stood waiting, their eyes on the area just beyond the end of the runway where the planes would emerge from the darkening scud. Zero five five.

At that moment the runway lights came on, dim and washed-out in the greyness, two long lines leading to where the fire trucks had pulled up on the middle taxiway, then going beyond.

Four miles out, the controller was saying. Zero five one.

"The lights aren't up all the way," Dunning said.

Harlan, looking, gave a slight shrug.

"Call the tower," Dunning ordered.

Harlan picked up the phone. "What's their number, Major? Do you know?"

"Look it up."

"It's restricted. It's not in the book."

"Ask the operator."

Zero five one, still. Holding steady. Approaching the glide path. Zero five one.

"Come on, come on," Dunning commanded. "Ask the operator!"

Drifting slightly to the right. Left two more degrees. Ten feet above the glide path.

Harlan was arguing with the operator, "I know it's restricted. Just put me through. It's urgent."

Two and three-quarters miles from touchdown. Going slightly high again. Fifteen feet now. Zero four nine is your heading.

Dunning reached for the phone. "Listen, this is Major Dunning in mobile. We're having an emergency on the field! Get me the tower right away."

"Sir, it's res—"

"Just get me the tower!"

"May I have your name again, sir?"

"Dunning, goddamn it! Major Dunning!"

"Yes, sir, Major."

Tracking the right side. Twenty feet high on the glide path. Twenty-five. Still zero four nine. Now fifteen feet high. Coming back nicely. Ten. Back on glide path. Now going slightly low.

Hold it steady, Dunning said to himself.

Ten feet low. Now going to twenty. Bring it up. Thirty feet low.

Harlan at last had the tower. "They're turned all the way up now," he reported.

"Tell them to turn them down and then up again."

A mile and three quarters out. Holding forty feet low. The runway lights faded like guttering candles, nearly went out, then came up again.

"Not any brighter," Harlan said.

"All right. Tell them to leave them like that."

A mile and a half. Approaching GCA minimums. Left to zero four seven. Make that further left to zero four five.

Big corrections at the last moment. Dunning was looking hard at the clouds as headlights came up alongside and a figure hurried towards them from the car. It was Colonel Cadin, the fighter group commander. He pushed into the mobile.

Holding forty feet low. Off slightly to the right. Zero four five. Make that zero four zero. Passing through GCA minimums.

"What's going on, Bud?" Cadin said. "Who's up there?"

Suddenly Godchaux's arm flew up, pointing, and in the same instant the planes appeared, sinking through the clouds.

"They're not lined up," Godchaux said.

"You're off to the right!" Dunning called on the radio.

They were a hundred feet wide of the runway, breaking in and out of the heavy bottoms, slipping from sight, then reappearing. They began a bank towards the runway as they passed overhead, the noise loud and condensed, and a moment later vanished in the clouds.

"You're too long, White," Dunning called. "You're way too long."

They were in sight again, crossing over the lights about a third of the way down, still in a turn. They were not trying to land. They were trying to stay beneath and come around again.

"Stay on your instruments, White!" Dunning warned. "It's too low!"

"I have the runway."

"Who is that?" Cadin asked.

"Stay on your instruments!" Dunning called.

They shot through cloud whisps, still low, appearing, disappearing, spread apart a little and both, from the dark smoke, carrying a lot of power.

"I've lost you, White," Dunning called. "Do you still have the runway?"

Silence.

"Watch it, White. Fly your instruments, boy. It's too low."

There was a fragment that sounded like, ". . . no good," and soon after, "climbing up."

Dunning felt a moment of relief despite himself, knowing it was not over, it would be worse, the relief one has with a dying man who begins to breathe smoothly.

"Who is that?" Cadin said.

"A lieutenant. Cassada. Isbell's radio is out. He's got him on his wing."

"Can you send them to an alternate?"

"All the alternates are down. They don't have the fuel."

"What are they doing clearing into here with weather like this?" Cadin demanded. He was a full colonel, a year younger than Dunning.

"I wish I knew."

"Ah, Bud," Cadin said. "Jesus."

Over the air then, almost casually, came the question, "Do you have White Two?"

"Negative, White Lead," Dunning said. "Did you lose him?"

There was no reply. Dunning saw Godchaux's and Harlan's faces, expressionless, turned towards him. Not that far off, across the shadowy grass, he could see the lights of his office still on. It was ages ago that he had been sitting there. For a moment, he could not think.

"White Lead," he called, "are you still with White Two?"

It was like a courtroom, the icy question hung in the air. The controller was asking calmly, "Do you request another approach, White?"

"I'm separated from White Two," came the reply. "Do you have him on your scope?"

"You're separated from your wingman?"

"Affirmative. Do you have him?"

"Stand by," the controller said.

The clouds were dark now, solid as ice floes. Halfway down the runway the noiseless red lights of the waiting fire trucks were flashing. The sun had gone down, unseen. The day had ended. Dunning could sense it, feel it in his bones.

Isbell walked out of his office, turning off the light. It was early evening but still bright. He went down the hallway towards the back door. The building was empty, he could tell from the sound of his footsteps. The typewriters were silent, the adding machine.

In front of the bulletin board he stopped to read the notices. Under TEMPORARY was a photograph someone had clipped after they'd gotten back from Tripoli, curled at the edges but still there, a chimpanzee in goggles riding a motor scooter, and printed beneath: *Just let me have a decent airplane, Captain — I'll murder it.* Isbell had never seen Cassada looking at it, but there was no doubt he'd seen it. He had become more removed, his pride drawn tighter around him, buttoned at the collar.

Outside it was May dusk. Everyone had gone, the hardstand was empty. A stillness had fallen. A lone car came along the taxiway from the hangar, someone from maintenance who waved as they passed and turned down towards the gate, red taillights flashing on as they stopped and the guard came out to motion them by.

Across the base, in the housing area, the banks of lights were beginning to show. They would grow brighter as the buildings themselves faded. In the end they would float through the darkness, freed, like a liner at sea. Isbell stood for a while. He could smell the wetness in the earth, the world turning green. Each day it seemed stronger.

Far to the east, toward Mannheim, the sky was a scrawl of white tracings brilliant in the last light. The final encounters. He watched them as they slowly faded and disappeared, lopsided circles falling off into vertical drops. A last pair, fresh, were moving across the distant sky—Canucks probably, out of Zweibrücken. Slow as an eclipse they sped along, pencil thin, seeking.

Everything was quiet. The boulevards of the field were deserted, the intersections empty. It had been a day. It had been clear since dawn. Everybody had been up, searching like foxes, eager to meet. Up and over they had rolled in dogfights, filled with excitement, the ground above their heads, smoke rising blue from the towns, heaven beneath their feet. They had fought the crazy Canucks. They had fought the other groups and squadrons, they had fought one another, landing and hurrying in afterwards to shout about triumphs.

He stood complete and weary. He felt content. The last two contrails had straightened out. The Canadians were heading west again, going home to sneak in just before dark.

† † † † † † † † † †

"Well, this is a surprise."

Outside the store, Godchaux turned.

"Oh, hello, Mrs. Dunning."

She shook her head slightly. "I thought I told you about that."

"Mayann," Godchaux managed to say.

"What in the world are you doing here?"

Godchaux gestured towards the interior which was tiled in white. "Buying mussels," he said. "I told Jackie Grace I was coming down here and I'd get some for her."

Mayann Dunning made a face. "I'd rather eat pigs' feet," she said. "How do you cook them?"

"Gee, I don't know. She's going to cook them. I'm supposed to get three pounds. I was coming to Trier anyway, so I just . . ."

"Coming to Trier to do what?"

"Just look around."

"Look around for what?"

She had looked at him many times, in fact it was difficult not to look at him, but she had never had the opportunity with no one around. His skin was smooth and clear, his eyebrows dark but fine. Feeling her stare, in defense he smiled. His teeth!

"Where'd you get your eyelashes?" she said.

"I don't know." He gave an embarrassed shrug. "They just came."

"I'll come in with you while you get the mussels."

"I was going to get them on the way back."

"You don't want me to come in with you."

"No, it'd be fine. I was just not going to do it right now."

"Well, I'll come with you while you're doing whatever else you're doing."

"Just walking around."

"Jackie's cooking dinner?" Mayann asked as they walked.

"Yes, ma'am. We're all going over there."

"That's nice. She takes care of the bachelors in the flight."

"I guess she does."

"Sews on your buttons."

"She doesn't do that."

"Who does?"

She liked talking to him. Perhaps she would never really talk to him, but it was pleasant trying.

They walked on. Trier was an old town of dark red brick, a town dating back to Roman times. It was historically important but not particularly interesting. There were the remains of a large amphi-theater somewhere—Mayann had gone with the wives' club to see it—some Roman baths, and vineyards up in the hills.

"I'm hungry," Mayann said. "What time is it?"

"Almost twelve-thirty."

"Do you want some lunch."

In a restaurant with windows of brownish glass in rows of small circles, Godchaux ordered a beer.

"Do you like the local wine?" Mayann asked.

"Moselle, you mean? I've tried it. It's all right."

"Then you don't like it?"

"I guess I like the beer more."

"You know what I always say. I always say you should have what you want." She was opening the menu. "But only . . ."

He waited, slightly nervous. He could not imagine what she was going to add.

"Only after you know what you want."

The waitress was nearby. Godchaux said to her, "I'll have the wine."

"Moselle?"

"*Ja,* Moselle. Another glass of Moselle."

It was yellowish when it came. He drank it without much enthusiasm but ended up having a second glass of it.

"Have you ever played this?" Mayann said. She was laying out matches she had torn from a book of them. They formed a pyramid, five matches in the bottom row, three in the next, then one. Godchaux shook his head.

"No," he said.

The rules, she explained, were simple. From any one row any number of matches could be removed. Then it was the other player's turn, and so forth. The loser was the one who picked up the last match.

"You go," she said.

Godchaux looked at the matches for a minute or two and picked up the single match. Mayann picked up two from the row of five. Godchaux casually picked up the remaining three from the same row. That left three matches in what had been the middle row. Mayann picked up two of them.

"I get it," he said.

She laid them out again. This time he looked longer at the matches and picked up one from the row of five. She took away two from the same row. Godchaux took away one from the row of three. Mayann picked up the lone match from the top row.

Godchaux sat examining the situation. He saw he had lost again. If he picked up one or both matches from either row, she would remove both from the other row or just one.

"You win," he said. "Is there a trick to it?"

"No trick."

"There must be some trick."

"What makes you think so?"

"You always win."

The waitress was bringing their order.

"Not always," Mayann said. "You look like someone who wins."

He glanced up. She was not looking at him but at the plate being put before her.

"*Danke schoen,*" she said to the waitress.

"How did you and the major meet?" Godchaux said as he began to eat.

"We met in college."

"Before he went to flying school."

"I was pregnant when he went to flying school."

"Oh, you were already married."

"No."

"Oh."

"I was pregnant," she said, "but I took care of it like a good girl."

Godchaux didn't know what to say. He nodded a little vaguely and, stealing a glance at her, continued to eat.

"Bud thinks the world of you, I guess you know that."

Godchaux said nothing.

"He thinks . . . well, what do I need to tell you that for? Don't you want to know what *I* think?"

She had often teased him. She did not seem to be teasing now.

"Yeah," he said, admiring her.

"Don't you already know?"

Trier was a port town, on the Moselle, and possessed, though neither of them had heard of it, a celebrated garment said to be the robe of Christ. It was not ordinarily on display and was brought out only rarely, when it attracted great crowds. Close to the well-preserved Roman gate was the chief hotel of the town. It had survived the war undamaged—Trier was not heavily bombed—and was comfortable if a little old-fashioned. In such hotels one expected comfort. The hallways were wide and the doors of the rooms, which were large and seemed to have too much space, were glossy with a perfect, almost plastic coat of white.

The hotel was the Porta Nigra, named for the Roman gate. It was there, not only on that day but on a number thereafter that Lancelot, aware of the danger, went with his queen.

The clouds were spread in all directions like a layer of curdled milk. Far above them flew two Canadians looking, as always, for a fight. No one else was up, however, and they had turned homeward when, at the very last, they saw two contrails, lower, distant, to the south.

"Let's get those."

"I'm down to twelve hundred pounds," the wingman said.

"That's plenty."

They began a slow turn to bring themselves over and behind, and then rolled down. It was perfect. They hadn't been seen. As they closed they saw the big droptanks, bathtubs. Americans. Four hundred knots. Almost in range. Suddenly the two planes in front of them pulled up together in a left turn and disappeared into the glare of the sun. The Canadian leader held up his thumb to cover it and then his entire hand. He didn't see them. He continued to block out the sun, waiting for them to come out on one side of the glare or the other. Leveling out, he kept looking and heard his wingman call, "Eight o'clock!"

He strained to look back, over his shoulder. Sure enough, there they were.

"Hard left!" he called.

They began a tightening circle, turning amid their own contrails, which were persistent and thick. In the end the two opposing leaders were heading straight down, speed brakes out, canopy to canopy, rolling around each other like a barber pole. Through the very top of the canopy the Canadian could look into the other cockpit and see the pilot's head there, thrown back too. They were that close, absolutely vertical, the rate of descent needle straight down, the altimeter spinning like a wheel. Around and around, headed for the clouds until just above them they pulled out and began scissoring, almost in a stall, noses high, lurching past each other.

Slowly, sweat pouring from him, the Canadian began, because of the tanks, to get the better of it, skimming over the cloud surface. Suddenly, out of the corner of his eye he caught sight of the second American, come from he didn't know where and unbelievably close, the intake as big as a piano. Without pausing he pushed over and into the clouds.

He was safe there, unfollowable. He made several turns and at the end climbed out again, half expecting to see them waiting like terriers over a rat hole, but they were gone. He couldn't see them anywhere, nor his wingman. He called but got no answer. Only when he was nearly back to the base at Gros Tenquin did he get the wingman to reply.

"What happened to you?"

"I lost you when we went below the cons," the wingman said.

"I'll say you did."

The victors of the combat in which they had been matched against cleaner airplanes landed low on fuel in light rain. The ceiling had come down. The leader—it was Grace—was summoned from the locker room almost immediately. Isbell had learned from the servicing crew how much fuel had been left in the planes.

"Debrief later," he told Grace. "I want to talk to you."

"Yes, sir," said Grace in a serious voice, his flying suit dark where he'd been sweating beneath his parachute.

The door closed behind them.

In the briefing room, Godchaux waited, biting at the corner of a fingernail and looking at the floor. When somebody asked him a question he answered with only a grin. He bit at his fingernail again.

"Pretty close on, eh, Captain?" Abrams said in some confidence to Wickenden.

"Too close."

"Boy, oh, boy."

"I wouldn't talk about it," Wickenden said. "You start talking about it and the first thing you'll have the group commander down here wanting to know what's been going on."

"Captain," Abrams said, wounded, "I wouldn't say anything. You know that."

"Just so you understand."

"Sir, I'd never say a word."

"Just forget it. Make believe it never happened, that's the best thing." The door to Isbell's office had been closed for nearly fifteen minutes. "Staying up there like that to tangle with someone, knowing what the weather was," Wickenden declared. "Plain stupidity."

And a flight commander, he refrained from saying. Ought to be grounded, as well as that clown Godchaux, in there where the rest of them were coming in wanting to hear about it. Experience, he once told Wickenden, that was the thing. Correct. Using his head once in a while, that was the experience he needed. Just occasionally. Once a month, maybe. Even that would make a difference.

It was like an infection. Wickenden could see it spread. He could pick out the next one to do something brainless even if he'd never happened to lay eyes on him before. It was all over his face. "Captain, I can fly the airplane."

"Oh, is that it?"

"Yes, sir."

"Maybe so. Every fool says that."

"I'm not a fool."

"You don't have to be, but that doesn't mean you won't act like one."

"I'm not a fool," Cassada had said.

After a while the door opened and Grace came out, head bent forward a little as if in submission, lips compressed like a schoolboy. As he passed he looked at Wickenden and raised his eyebrows to show some sort of regret. In the briefing room Godchaux wanted to know if he was next. "Me?"

Grace shook his head. He took Godchaux by the arm and led him away from the others. They stood in a corner of the room.

"What did he say?"

Grace bent and took a light from Godchaux's cigarette. "We were too low on fuel, that was basically it. He's right, too."

"I'll say he is."

"Exactly how much did you shut down with? I told him four hundred pounds. He said it was lower."

"About half that."

"Well, that *is* low. That's much too low," Grace said as if there was no way for him to have known.

"What did you have?" Godchaux asked.

"I wasn't that bad off. I was low, but not that low."

"Like how much?"

"I was low."

"But what did you have?"

"Three hundred," Grace said.

Godchaux grinned at him.

"No, you weren't that bad off," Godchaux said. "Do you suppose those Canucks ever made it back all right?"

"I don't know. Maybe one of them did."

"What do you mean?"

They were both grinning.

"One of them is probably still hiding in the clouds," Grace said.

"I was about two hundred feet behind him. Even closer. I actually saw him turn his head and look back at me."

"Jesus, it was perfect."

Isbell was standing in the doorway to his office. He may even have been able to hear it. He knew Wickenden was looking at him. He went back inside and closed the door.

Down the hallway, near the latrine, was a sign that said flying was inherently safe but, like the sea, unforgiving. Wickenden, standing there, was able to hear Cassada, dog-eager, asking Godchaux if he had used flaps to scissor. Godchaux illustrated with his hands. "Right here," he said, "I swapped them, brakes in, flaps down."

Cassada was nodding. Wickenden walked past without seeming to pay attention. Afterwards he motioned to Cassada. "Come here a minute," he said.

They stood by the blackboard. The room by then was empty. Wickenden looked down at the floor. "I've been in three other squadrons," he said.

"Yes, sir."

"This is your first, isn't it?"

"Yes, sir."

"Sometimes the first is the last one."

Cassada said nothing. Though it was a matter of only eight or nine years, he seemed much younger standing there. He seemed a different, unrelated breed.

Wickenden went on, as if thinking back, "I had a pilot in my flight you remind me of. Back at Turner. You're a lot like him. You want to know how?"

Cassada remained silent. Wickenden raised his eyes.

"You couldn't tell him anything. He was too smart for that. He knew too much."

"That's not me, Captain."

"One day I let him go out alone, just local, and about ten miles away from the field he started some low-level acrobatics. Unauthorized, naturally. He dished out of the first roll. Went straight in."

Cassada was returning his look, almost with a kind of pity.

"You could have put what was left of him in a matchbox," Wickenden said.

"So?"

"I knew all along it was going to happen. I just didn't know how. Or when."

"Is that it?"

"No, that's not it. I want you to draw a lesson from that."

"What kind of lesson?"

"You know what kind."

Cassada nodded somewhat tentatively. A pilot like Grace was what he wanted to be, a pilot everyone respected, who had flown in combat and been shot at, who'd been hit by ground fire like Grace and brought the airplane back somehow, a man you could count on.

"You couldn't tell him anything," Wickenden repeated.

"That's not me."

"You think not?"

"No, sir, and I'm going to be alive after you are."

Wickenden's face hardened.

"Never happen," he said grimly.

The flight commanders' meeting was always at the end of the month, a discussion of concerns and of what things were coming up, ending with Isbell asking each of them directly about any particular problems. Wickenden sat without saying a word, looking bored.

"Nothing?" Isbell said.

"No."

Isbell knew the truth. Wickenden was waiting for the others to leave, the lesser others. At last they did and Wickenden stayed behind, his mouth in a thin line, staring down at his hands and working the Zippo lighter, open and shut. At last he said, "I know you don't want to hear this, but it's not going to go away."

"What's that?"

"Cassada."

"What's wrong? What's he done?"

Wickenden opened and clapped his lighter closed several times. Finally he said, "It's not what he . . . It's what he's going to do."

"Have an accident."

"He's going to kill himself. I know what I'm talking about. I had another one just like him, in the States."

"The low-level acrobatics."

"That's right," Wickenden said. When he spoke, everything was final. It was like someone beating a carpet, flat, heavy blows. "You could have put what was left of him in that ashtray."

"I suppose you told Cassada the story."

"Certainly."

Isbell could imagine it. Maybe you don't think so, but I've had them like you before. The difficulty was that once you said I can't do anything with you, what was left after that? It was an ultimate statement.

"Well, I had my doubts about putting him in your flight. I didn't want to put him with Grace or the others. You'll just have to make it your job to keep him from killing himself."

"Nobody can do that," Wickenden said.

"They can't?"

"He has the mark of death on him."

"Oh, my foot."

Wickenden began clapping his lighter shut again.

"The mark of death," Isbell said. "You once told me the same thing about Dumfries."

"It's true."

"You're getting to see it in everybody. Look at me, do I have it, too? If I don't, I'm going to be worried."

Wickenden had his eyes on the lighter held in his lap, lifting the lid and snapping it down. He knew certain things. Nothing could change them.

"You know more about flying than he does, don't you?" said Isbell.

"Yes."

"You spent four years," Wickenden's eyes shot up at this, alert at the number, "learning leadership among other things, didn't you? They were still teaching that up there, weren't they?" He could see Wickenden taking the inside of his cheeks between his teeth. "Well, weren't they?"

"You know just what they teach."

"I should."

Wickenden clapped it again.

"You're the senior flight commander," Isbell said. "Ops officer is the next step. If I weren't here you'd probably be ops officer. You'd be telling your flight commander the same thing: take care of this man. Find a way."

Silence.

"What more do you want?" Isbell asked.

"All right, sir." He was chewing on the walls of his mouth. The three words were an ancient, a cadet formula.

"Who else should I give him to?"

Wickenden sat motionless.

"Who would you suggest?"

"It wouldn't matter who you gave him to. There's a hierarchy ..."

"A what?"

"A hierarchy of knowing."

"What is this, some Eastern religion?"

"And he doesn't know where he is in it. He won't ever know."

Isbell rubbed his ear and seemed as if he might sigh. Without another word Wickenden got up to go. Isbell nearly stopped him but they had been through things before. There came a point where nothing that was said made a difference. Wickenden would stand silently, wearing intransigence like a coat of arms.

He walked out the door.

"Wick!" Isbell called, the tone half apology.

But Wickenden chose not to hear.

Late in the fall ten planes went to Munich again to take over the alert from Pine's squadron which had been there a month. There was, for a moment, the lapping of two cultures, a few words here and there, a greeting, a taunt. Squadrons were distinct. They were identical and unique. Pine had been known, when asked for a favor by a rival squadron, to say, what do I get in return?.

Isbell, one foot on a chair, was being briefed and taking some notes, perhaps the name of a bar or a couple of telephone numbers he would post later. As soon as Pine and the rest of them left, he pointed to a broom in the corner. Phipps picked it up and began sweeping. Outside, the first engines of the departing planes were being started. Cassada, the pale imprint of an oxygen mask still on his face, kneeled with the dustpan. Isbell had gone.

"That's right, lady," Cassada muttered, "I'm a jet pilot."

"Hold it flatter," Phipps said.

In the barracks they dragged their bags along the wide hallway and banged open doors. At the far end there was an empty room.

Phipps arrived first. In the top drawer of a bureau there were still matches, coat checks, halves of tickets—weeks of someone's pockets emptied at two in the morning. Phipps was throwing them into the wastebasket when Dumfries appeared.

"Anybody in here yet?"

"No one but me," Phipps said.

"Don't you want the lights on?"

"What? No, leave them off. Cassada may be coming."

Dumfries gave a confused smile and struggled in with his bag. He stood looking at the empty beds and finally chose one against the wall. He dropped his things on it and brushed himself off.

"They're not all moved out yet," he said.

"I know."

"I heard Captain Pine say some of them were going to stay over for the weekend."

"Is that so?"

"They must like it down here."

"I guess they do." Munich. The blue twilight, trollies rocking along the streets and shop windows coming alight.

"I'd want to go straight home. A month, that's long enough."

"If it's the same as last time they'll probably have to go through town with a press gang to get them out of here."

"With what?"

"A press gang. You know what that is?"

"Oh, sure," Dumfries said. "I just didn't hear you."

He unzipped one side of his bag and took out a framed photograph of his wife. She came from a very fine family, he had mentioned more than once. Her father was a dentist. By profession, as Dumfries put it. They had carpet even on the stairs.

He put the photograph on top of the bureau, then dug into the side compartment and found his hairbrushes. He placed them beside the photograph. They were better for you than a comb, he had told Phipps.

"Why is that?"

"Have you ever seen a bald horse?"

"A bald horse?"

"It's because they brush them."

Phipps watched as Dumfries unpacked and put his clothes away, drawer by drawer, hiding his camera among the undershirts. The Russians must have them, too, Phipps decided. That was the only reassuring thing. He could almost imagine it, steep, terrifying battles high over Berlin and all the Eugenes crying their pitiful I've lost you's, turning hopelessly through the confusion and heading off in the wrong direction.

Through the doorway then, holding in front of him a single bag as taut from things inside as a sausage skin, came Cassada, the bag hitting his knees as he moved. He reached out in passing and switched on the light. Dumfries straightened up, startled. Cassada looked from one of them to the other. "What are you doing, saving electricity?" he said.

He dropped his bag. "This is great, being down here, isn't it?" He began to pull things out of the bag, dropping them everywhere, looking for something. Finally he took hold of a towel and snaked it out and around his neck.

"What do you think about going into town?" he asked, sitting down and hooking his finger into his bootlaces, jerking them loose.

"How?" Phipps said.

"Drive. I had an airman in maintenance drive my car down."

"Yeah, maybe. I'm going to eat here anyway," Phipps said.

"Me, too," said Dumfries.

"What for?" Cassada asked, still trying to find something. "We can eat in town. You have any soap?" he finally said.

"Is that what you've been looking for?"

"Here," Dumfries said.

"Toss it."

Cassada trapped it against his chest with one hand and went to shower.

Phipps and Dumfries walked to the club. It was just becoming dark. The trees had some wind in them. The branches quivered. A good-looking cashier, a girl with a downturned mouth, was still working at the club, counting out money from the cash drawer with long fingers, converting military scrip into deutsche marks. She wore a thin, gold wedding band, perhaps to deflect questions.

Dumfries hesitated in front of her. "Hi, Marianne," he said. Unsure of how to continue, he examined the movie schedule posted there, his belly stuck out like a brewer's. "We just got down here today," he said. "We took over from the 72nd."

She nodded but did not comment. Dumfries thought of something.

"Say, remember that wine you once told me about? Spot-lease? Well, I tried some of that."

"Oh, yes?"

"It was good. Boy, I like good wine. That's one thing about Europe." He was smiling like a jazzman, a meaningless smile.

In the bar, in the dim light the pilots sat together. The dice were rattling.

"Hey, Phipps. Come on, you want to play?"

"You can't lose in a big game," someone said.

"Where's Roberto?"

Cassada was known as a demon player given to wild calls.

"He went into town."

"Already?"

Dumfries came in after a while and sat beside Phipps.

"She's a nice girl," he said.

"The cashier? What makes you think she's nice?"

"I've talked to her. I just think she's nice. Most of these fellows don't even know what a decent German girl is like."

"Some of them know."

Dumfries began to talk about the maid they had, he and Laurie, how nice she was. He described her habits, her love of cleanliness and visits to her parents. She was very shy. As Phipps half-listened he suddenly realized what it was about Dumfries: nothing bored him. And calling the tight-skirted cashier, owner of a siren's body, nice. She may have been a lot of things but nice was not one of them. Cassada was probably already driving to town. Phipps wished he'd gone, too.

In the early morning, before daylight, Isbell walked alone through the hangar past the planes being repaired, broken in two by the mechanics, the lines hanging loose, bleeding black into drip pans. The hangar lights were on though no one yet was working.

In the ready room Wickenden was posting his schedule as the members of his flight sat watching. Isbell stood near his shoulder for a few moments, unnoticed, then took the rag as Wickenden was writing and rubbed out the leader of the first two, Phipps, replacing it with his own name next to Cassada's. Wickenden didn't say anything. He kept on writing. Cassada sat stretched out in unconcern, his neck on the back of a chair and his legs in the G-suit chaps resting straight with only his heels touching the floor, doing everything he could not to look like the others. He'd watched Isbell without moving his head, out of the corner of his eye. It was just the way Godchaux sat.

Isbell said nothing to him but went into the next room, picked up his things and took them out to the ship. To the east it was becoming light, a great, forlorn light that seemed to sweep in from the steppes. The air was still, a sea-like calm. He laid his parachute against one of the wheels and began to walk around the airplane, starting at one wing and then following the fuselage to the tail, running a hand over the chilly skin as he went, sometimes patting it like a horse as if to calm it. He was entering the realm of his true authority. He had barely finished the walk-around when the horn sounded. He saw Cassada running out the door, pulling on his gloves as he went, the blare of the horn flooding around him, the crewmen coming after.

Quickly Isbell pulled on his parachute and climbed into the cockpit, fumbling for the safety belt buckles. The horn kept blowing in panic. The high whine of the engines starting began.

Off on the first scramble, early in the day, no finer time, cold and quiet, the smoke coming straight up from the towns. Munich was blue, deserted. The roads seemed dusted with chalk. The trains were running empty, the streetcars.

At altitude it was silent. The controller directed them north. Serene, pure as angels they flew. At Ingolstadt some clouds began, a thin, floating fence that went up towards Berlin, grey as a river. Cassada was in position just where he was meant to be, off to the left, looking past Isbell towards the sun and the unknown east. It was there the enemy lay, sometimes inactive, sometimes flying themselves on a parallel course waiting for the slightest violation of the invisible border, or lurking below the contrails, unseen. The controller would call them out but not always, and when the ground was covered by clouds there was always the slight chance of error, a mistake in position or which radar blip was which. The threat of the unexpected was always there. Come and get us, Isbell thought to himself. We're here in the open, alone. Bring us down. Try.

There was nothing, though. No targets, the controller advised. They flew almost to Frankfurt and then turned back. Cassada's plane went from black, to gun color, to silver as he swung from one side to the other in the brilliant light.

They had spoken hardly a word. The earth lay immense and small beneath them, the occasional airfields white as scars. Down across the Rhine. The strings of barges, smaller than stitches. The banks of poplar. Then a city, glistening, struck by the first sun. Stuttgart. The thready streets, the spires, the world laid bare.

A light mist was still rising off the fields when they landed. They walked in together.

"What a day!" Cassada said.

Isbell agreed. His body felt empty. His mind was washed clean.

"Ingolstadt," Cassada said. "Have you ever noticed Ingolstadt, passing over?"

Isbell nodded. "They're all different. They have their own shapes. Some of them you can recognize just seeing part of, through a hole in the clouds. Ingolstadt's like that."

"I look down and think how I'd like to be there—even if I don't really want to. Do you know what I mean? You've . . . have you ever been there?"

"A couple of times."

"What's it like?"

"I don't know," Isbell said. "It's not as great as it was this morning."

Cassada was looking around, taking things in with his sea-blue eyes, the flawless day.

"You could say that about everyplace," he commented.

It was true, Isbell thought, exactly. He felt a desire to reply in kind. It was not often you found anyone who could say things.

"You're flying a good wing, Robert," he said.

"I guess I ought to be."

"What does that mean?"

"I've had enough practice."

"Don't be too impatient," Isbell said. "Just be ready. You know Napoleon's maxim: every soldier carries a marshal's baton in his knapsack."

There was a silence.

"Whatever that means," Cassada said.

They went to breakfast in the small dining room behind the kitchen at the club. The waitress was sleepy. It was not much past seven. They played with the forks, not talking, waiting to be served. In the air was the warm smell of food.

"It's been a year or more, hasn't it?" Isbell said.

Cassada pressed a tine into the tablecloth.

"Yes, sir," he said.

"It doesn't seem it."

"No?"

"Seems longer to you?"

"Some of it's been great," Cassada said. "The flying. Gunnery."

"So, what is it you're not getting?"

"I've learned some things."

"I'm sure you have. You're going to get your chance," Isbell said. "Don't worry. It'll come."

"Yes, sir. I know. It's in my knapsack or something."

"You're going to win. You'll win big one day."

"You think so?"

"Everything you want."

Cassada was pressing a small square into the tablecloth, two parallels, then connecting them.

"Captain," he said, "it was great flying with you today. All I want is for someone around here, someone with authority, to have a little confidence in me, that's all."

"I have confidence in you. Just be ready."

"For what?"

"For everything you expect to be."

"You amaze me, Captain."

"Why?"

"It's nothing like that. We're talking about two different things. I don't know. I just don't understand, I guess."

There was suddenly a great deal Isbell wanted to say. They could have talked. They could have pushed the plates aside and leaned forward on their elbows, talking while the dust floated sideways through bolts of sunshine and the eggs turned cold, but it didn't quite happen. The moments don't fulfill themselves always. Somehow they started eating in silence and it was impossible to begin.

Phipps came running out into the cold, looking around frantically. Damn it, he thought—the lot was empty. There was one car. He ran towards it.

"Hey, hold up!" he shouted, struggling to get his arm in the flight jacket sleeve. Exhaust was coming up in back of the car. He tried to open the door. It was locked. He beat on the window with his palm.

Cassada reached across and unlocked the door. Phipps slid in beside him.

"Thanks. I was afraid everybody had gone. Jesus, this seat's cold."

Cassada was working the choke to get the engine warmed up. Minutes went by, it seemed.

"We're going to be late," Phipps said.

"We'll make it." Cassada looked sleepy. His eyes were red.

"It's four minutes till."

"I know."

He began to back up, rolling the window down to see. He pulled onto the road and rubbed at the frosted windshield with his fist. Hunched over, looking through a slit of clear glass at the bottom, the width of a pencil, he began to drive. Phipps, wiping at the windshield himself, said, "We're not going to make it at this rate."

Cassada speeded up a little.

"Can you see?" Phipps said.

"It's the back I'm worried about. I can't tell if anyone's behind us."

"Take a chance."

Cassada shifted into third.

"I don't want to get a ticket," he said. "The major pulls your license."

"You won't need a license if we're late."

They began to go faster. Phipps looked at his watch.

"Open it up, Robert. We've got two minutes."

The clear area on the glass was growing bigger. As they turned past the end of the runway they were doing forty-five.

"I'm just waiting to hear a siren," Cassada murmured.

Phipps rolled down the window to look back.

"There's nobody."

They were going fifty.

"About a minute and a half," Phipps warned.

"I know."

"Come on."

"They'll throw us in jail. It's a twenty-five-mile limit."

"I tell you nobody's behind us."

The heater was finally beginning to work. Phipps sniffed the warming air.

"What have you been carrying in this car? Flowers?"

"What?"

"It smells like it."

They had swerved in behind the hangar. The doors flew open and they ran for it. As they sat down, Isbell looked at his watch.

"That's cutting it pretty close," he commented.

Cassada was sitting at the end of the first row, head down. He glanced up but did not answer. His head was down later, too, when Wickenden gathered the flight. Cassada listened like a boxer between rounds, head bent forward, hands dropped loosely between his thighs, as if his manager were telling him things there was no sense paying attention to, in thirty seconds he'd be in there alone again. He yawned with his mouth closed.

It was perfume, thought Phipps suddenly. That was the smell.

"You must be making out all right in Munich," he said to Cassada later.

"Munich? Yeah, it's a good town."

"Where do you go?"

"I'll tell you sometime."

The truth was he wandered around Munich at night. He went to the Regina Bar, the Bongo, the Coliseum once or twice. He hadn't the money or time to cut a swath and in fact had not found a girl. The perfume was from a girl he'd driven home, a girl he would never want to be seen with.

Still, Munich freed him. He went in with Godchaux sometimes though usually Godchaux had a date. One night he met a woman who was divorced and had lived in the States and even for a while had a job there. She was a fabric designer and shared an apartment with her mother. The mother was not in the apartment that night. They sat on the couch—it was actually a daybed with small pillows—and talked. Suddenly she leaned over and kissed him as a man might do. Cassada was a little drunk—they'd met in a bar. He felt her hand slip inside his clothes. He said nothing.

"You're very excited," she whispered.

It was silent for a while. He began hurriedly to unbutton her dress but suddenly it was too late. She made a sound like inhaling and withdrew her hand.

"Do you have a handkerchief?" she asked.

He'd seen her several times after that though he was not really attracted to her—she talked only about her mother and herself— and then near the end of an evening in a place called the Elysée he stood near a girl at the top of the stairs that led down to the *Damen* and *Herren*. She had a Slavic face though he did not recognize it as such, wide across the cheeks, and cropped dark hair. He stared at her.

"You probably don't speak English, but so what?" he said impulsively.

She looked at him.

"My name is Robert. I just thought you look great standing there and you have a terrific face."

"You, too," she said.

He was stunned into silence, but something had happened. It was as if they were at a dance, she seemed to accept his invitation, to nod yes. Her face was singular. It possessed a light or perhaps it was clarity.

"I didn't know you understood what I was saying."

"If you knew, what would you have said?"

"I'd say, I hope you're not leaving. I . . . I'd like to listen to you for a while."

"To listen to me?" She gave a slight smile. "That wouldn't be so interesting."

"I'll make a bet."

"A bet?"

"It's too hard to explain. You live in Munich?"

"Yes."

"Me, too."

"In Munich?"

"Well a little outside Munich. Fürstenfeldbruck."

"So, you're a pilot."

They were words Cassada loved. Everyone that didn't know anything about this.

"Yeah. I'm a fighter pilot."

"Maybe I could guess it."

"How could you guess it?"

She shrugged.

"So, listen. What's your name?"

"I don't think so," she said.

"No, what is it, really? Tell me. I'm absolutely serious, you have the face I've been looking for."

"It's no good to tell you my name."

"Yes, it is."

"Karen."

"Karen," he repeated. "Are you married? You're not married or anything?"

"You're so intense."

"No, tell me."

"What do you want to know again?"

She was very good-looking, her cheekbones and white teeth.

"Where'd you learn to speak English?" he said and before she could answer, "That's really lucky. But you know something?"

"Yes," she said.

"Yes, what?"

"I know something."

She smiled and Cassada did also. It was a pleasure to talk to her. She spoke the same language, exactly. It would go back and forth between them. He would know her. Someone was coming up the stairs then—Cassada barely noticed—until an arm was put through hers, a man's arm.

"Hey," Cassada protested and then saw in disbelief who it was. He was unable to speak.

"Ready?" Isbell said to the girl.

"Wait a minute," Cassada said. "What's going on?"

"We're leaving."

"I mean, what is this?"

"What is it? What do you think?"

"No, no. I was here. *I* met you, didn't I?" he said to the girl. She gave a slight laugh.

"I'll see you, Robert," Isbell said.

"Hey, Captain. This is not on duty."

"Duty?"

"You can't pull rank."

"I don't have to."

"Let *her* choose."

"You're out past where you should be," Isbell said calmly.

"No, no. Oh, no."

"Let's go," Isbell said calmly to the girl. "See you later," he said to Cassada.

Cassada stood there. The one woman in Munich, he thought, the one woman in all that time. He felt sick. He could not believe it. He went out to the street after them, almost trembling, but too late, they were gone, the red taillights leaving him behind.

A lieutenant named Myers had been killed near Toul. The paper didn't give his name, just his group, but someone had learned it. It was the second accident of the week. There'd been a bailout over Kaiserslautern a few days before.

"Myers," Godchaux said. "I knew him. He was in my class in flying school. Good pilot."

Harlan was reading the paper.

"They all are," he said from in back of the pages.

"All are what?"

"Good pilots. Whatever happens to the lousy ones? That's what I wonder."

It was one of the reasons to read the *Stars and Stripes,* starting in with a kind of sweepstakes excitement, wondering if there'd be one and if it would be anyone they knew. Harlan wasn't that far off—it was sometimes the best ones. The best or the worst.

There was a wind blowing, a strong wind keening under the eaves and making a sound like a prayer call. Isbell stood by himself

at the window. He could see the wind in the clear air and the shifting tone of the grass. Six planes were up and he was waiting for
them to enter traffic. Not far from him Abrams sat squinting at the
tape in the adding machine, printed with hour upon hour of flying
time rich with error.

It was not that he was indifferent. He worked diligently, even
after hours, round face shining with effort. Isbell had made up his
mind more than once to get rid of him. It was hard to do. Some kind
of lazy loyalty had crept in.

In the hangar birds nested in the rafters, skimming in and out
the wide doorways. Isbell met Dunning there.

"Swallows," Dunning said.

"Is that what they are?"

"That's what they are, all right."

They were curving out into the brilliant day, swift, barely missing.

"They'll be crapping all over the windshields," Dunning commented.

There were a few planes there that maintenance was at work on.
Dunning stood peering up into the shadows.

"I'll have to get down here with a shotgun," he said.

"Wickenden could probably do it."

"I don't want anybody blowing holes in the roof. I'll do it
myself," Dunning said. "Well, they're after us again. We have to
send two pilots down to Tripoli. It's part of a meet to decide which
team from Europe will go to the States."

"To Vegas?"

"Yeah."

"We haven't practiced."

"We're not even in it," Dunning said. "It's a two-group shoot-
off."

"Which ones? How'd they pick them?"

Dunning was patting his pockets, looking for something.

"They did it from the gunnery scores," he said.

"And we're not in it?"

"Yeah, I'd like to see the scores."

"I can't believe it. They were probably punching holes in the targets with a screwdriver. I've seen that."

"Maybe we should have thought of that ourselves."

His pockets, as he fished in them, seemed too small. He felt around his thighs.

"I've got the orders here somewhere. Here we are. A flight leader to be one of the judges and one tow pilot."

"For how long?"

"Well, they don't say. About a week or more, I'd guess."

Isbell saw them returning, climbing down sun-browned from the cockpit.

"For the flight leader . . ." he said, considering.

"Reeves."

"He'd be all right."

"Who else do you think?"

"Me."

Dunning gave a slow, knowing smile. He inserted the meditative tip of his little finger in his ear and moved it around, looking at the floor and then at Isbell.

"It's only for a week," Isbell said. "Things are winding down here. We're going to be relieved on Saturday. Wick can run things."

"I suppose so."

Isbell waited.

"Who do you want to take with you?" Dunning asked. "It ought to be someone who'd get something out of going. A good gunner."

"Good or with good potential."

"There's Godchaux, of course. Dumfries didn't do so bad last time we were down."

"Not Dumfries," Isbell said. Dunning seldom agreed to two things in a row. It was necessary to edge around like a crab, come in from the side. "Let me think about it."

"All right. We have to send the names in today."

"Give me an hour or so."

It was cold in the hangar. The noon wind was cutting along the roof and making a strange, blue sound. The note rose and then faded, as if there were an empty bottle and the wind blowing across it.

"Roast chicken for lunch," Dunning said. "Have you been over?"

"Not yet."

"Better get there while there's some left."

"I'll be along."

Later, where the road passed the end of the runway Isbell stopped and waited at the red light while two of his planes landed, a little unsteady in the powerful wind. The Volksbus quivered, too, its flatness catching the wind. He saw the planes touch down and slow almost immediately. Finally, looking as if they'd stopped completely, they showed their sides as they turned off the runway halfway down. He heard a horn blow. Someone behind him accelerated impatiently past.

In the barracks the next day, Dumfries sat watching as Cassada packed, tossing clothes on top of the dresser like someone expelled from school.

"I hear you're going to Tripoli."

"That's right."

"How'd that happen?"

Cassada gave a shrug. "Captain Isbell told me I was going, that's all."

"What's it for?"

"A gunnery meet."

"Are you going to shoot?"

"I don't know. I hope so."

Dumfries sat flicking at a set of car keys on the table with his finger.

"I just wonder how they made the choice," he said.

"Captain Wickenden put me up for it."

"No, really."

"I'm serious."

"He wouldn't do that. I don't think he'd do that."

"He decided to reform."

Dumfries continued flicking the keys, his brow puzzled.

"Tell me the truth," he said.

# IV

HARLAN TURNS TO THEM, SUDDENLY POINTING . . .

† † † † † † † † † † †

Harlan turns to them, suddenly pointing.

"What?"

"Look out there, Major."

Dunning sees nothing.

"Where?" he says.

Harlan waves a finger back and forth, pointing all over. Godchaux looks, then raises a hand, palm up. On the window glass points of water are appearing. Suddenly Dunning sees them and understands. It almost seems a sign. He would give the world for just one thing, to have them both on the ground. The rain is the answer. The trees are darker now. The clouds are heavier, the daylight gone from them.

They don't have Isbell yet. They think he might be orbiting the beacon. Dunning turns that over in his mind. Would Isbell be doing that, circling up there, waiting for nothing while his last fuel goes? No, Dunning thinks, but what else might he do? He can't decide. If only Cadin weren't there.

"It's just coming down light, Major," Godchaux says from the doorway. "It isn't bad."

"No."

"It might even stop."

Dunning doesn't reply. Things that will never matter. White Lead is waiting for an answer, he wants to know if they have White Two yet. He wants to be steered to him.

"Listen, never mind about White Two," Dunning directs. "What's your fuel?"

"Say again, GCA."

"This is mobile. What's your fuel?"

After a moment,

"Seven hundred pounds."

Seven hundred pounds. Dunning imagines they can hear that all over the base, in the other squadrons, the headquarters, the housing area. The tape is running. Up in the tower it's all being recorded, static, squeals, voices. Everything that would be rerun again and again. Seven hundred pounds—the board would be writing it on their yellow tables, seven and two zeroes.

"Never mind about him, White," Dunning calls. "You'll never find him in the weather."

No answer.

"White Lead?"

There is nothing.

"Do you read mobile, White?"

"Roger."

"Make another approach. It's looking better down here. It's breaking up a little."

Cadin takes the mike.

"White Lead, this is Colonel Cadin. Stay cool. Never mind the weather, you can make it in."

"You were blocked. I couldn't read."

Cadin repeats his instruction and as he finishes they hear the end of something White is saying, ". . . clear on top."

"Where are you, White?" he asks.

"I'm climbing."

"You're not on top?"

"Tops are about nine thousand."

Dunning stands silent, trying to think. Things are running through his mind like a stream. They're both going to bail out. He has to get them down somehow, at least one of them. Godchaux shakes his head a little, looking at the ground. Harlan is watching the rain. It's not coming down harder, but neither is it letting up. The water shines on the roof of the Volksbus and around the runway lights. The runway will be slick. That's the least of it. No one's going to be using the runway, Harlan thinks. They could be parked right in the middle of it, as far as that goes. Dunning takes back the mike.

"White," he calls abruptly, "don't climb any higher. That's an order. Make another approach."

"I'm at forty-five hundred now," Cassada reports.

"Don't climb! Do you understand? Shoot another approach."

"I'm at five thousand, Major."

He is doing the unthinkable. His heart skidding wildly in his chest, he is spending the last of his fuel, like diving, though this is the opposite, with lungs bursting and no breath left, almost none, into the rolling dark water where he must try and find someone drowned. He is casting his own chances away, from either some fierce sense of duty or the confused desire to do what Isbell would have done, or perhaps be with him in disaster, the two of them at the last.

For a moment they are all persuaded. It's a slim chance but

somewhere up there Isbell is flying in silence. There's at least the chance of them seeing each other, joining and trying it together one last time.

"He don't have the fuel," Harlan says quietly.

They don't hear him or don't want to. There's always the last minute. You come to fields you've given up on, you knew you would never be able to find. At the last moment they appear magically as if summoned out of nothing. It could be like that.

"He don't have it to spare," Harlan warns.

Godchaux stands in the doorway hugging himself and looking outside. The beige felt shows under the turned-up collar of his blouse. He blows into the end of his fist to warm his fingers. He shakes his head again. His expression is calm but all this is amazing to him, unbelievable. It's already part of lore.

Dunning leans on the counter, staring out. The seat of his trousers is wrinkled from sitting all day, and the back of his jacket. One chance in a hundred is all, but still a chance. He brings the microphone to his mouth, ready to speak. His thumb fiddles with the button. Finally, unable to stay silent, he says,

"Are you on top yet, White?" He presses the button in and out to make sure he's transmitting. "White from mobile, are you on top yet?"

Harlan says nothing. He would like to say, what's the point of his going up? He's headed the wrong way. You don't get down by going up. You don't have to go to college to figure that out. The thing that's really too bad is they can't talk to each other. That would be nice, to hear them, Cassada and the captain, especially the next five minutes. Old Wickenden was right for once. They should of listened to him. Sometimes these regulars know what they're talking about. It's the law of averages.

"Fortify White from mobile," Dunning calls. He says it twice, then a third time, looking around at the cloud bases as he does.

Godchaux is blowing on his fingertips.

"Fortify White," Dunning says urgently, "do you read? White from mobile, do you read?"

Beneath the palms, someone was trying to start a weapons carrier. It was a full colonel, his head bent forward as he looked for the ignition switch in the dark.

"Chance of catching a ride with you?" Isbell asked.

"Who's that?" the colonel said, turning.

"Captain Isbell, Colonel."

"I'll see if we have room," he said and waved an arm at a group coming down the front steps of the club, holding on to each other and singing. "Let's go!" he called, looking for the switch again. "Goddamn champs! Let's go!"

They began climbing in. Isbell waited. The colonel was touching everything on the panel, feeling for the switch. "How's things in the old 5th?" he said to Isbell. "Bunch of hamburgers."

"We're doing all right, Colonel."

"Oh, yeah?" He glanced up and saw Piebes, winner of the air-to-air. "Get in here, you goddamn dead-eye," he said.

Piebes tried. He managed to lift one leg onto the running board.

He seemed to wonder about what to do next. He was wearing the colonel's hat, grinning, the silver streaks of lightning visible in the dark.

The colonel slapped the passenger seat beside him. "Sit down," he said.

"Aye, aye, sir," Piebes said, pulling himself in. His head hit the canvas roof. Somebody picked the hat up for him.

The colonel stiffened to find the starter with his foot and pushed down. The engine turned over a few times and caught weakly.

"Great equipment," he said. "Get aboard," he told Isbell.

The back was crowded, Isbell could see. "That's all right, we'll catch the bus."

"Make up your mind, for Christ's sake," the colonel said.

The weapons carrier backed up and then roared off without head-lights. Near the theater someone turned them on. As they passed some lights, the colonel could be seen bareheaded, Piebes in the hat.

Isbell walked back to where Cassada was standing. People were still coming out of the club. There was the sound of a woman's heels on the cement. It was too dark to see.

"Who was that, Colonel Neal? He seemed pretty happy," Cassada said.

"Famous figure."

"Why is that?"

"You know how old he is?" Isbell said.

"No."

"Thirty-four."

"Is that all?"

"He was one of the first men in his class to make bird."

They were alone in the darkness, beneath the stars.

"Major Dunning's older than that," Cassada remarked.

"Well, that happens, too. But he's in line for a promotion. His record's good."

"How old are you, Captain?"

"Thirty-one," Isbell said.

Cassada shook his head a little.

"It's a long pull, isn't it?" he said.

"Not for everybody," Isbell replied.

"Colonel Neal."

"He's not the only one."

"You'll get a squadron next."

"I might. I hope so. Not here. I'll be going home too soon. In the States, maybe."

"Well, let me know. I'd like to be in it," Cassada said.

"I'll come looking for you."

The bus came rattling up, headlights quivering before it. It was filled with airmen and NCOs. Isbell stood with Cassada in the back, at the end of a line of lolling heads and the slow reveal of faces as they passed a streetlight. A sergeant was talking. "Lieutenant," he recited, "I loaded them myself, that's what I told him." He had a hard, lined face. Isbell could see him as they went by the hospital.

"You know what he says to me? He says, Bonney, that's good enough for me. That's good enough for me, he says. I tell you, that means something when they talk to you like that."

The others were listening, turned sideways in the seats or leaning from above, holding on with one hand.

"I seen a lot of them," Bonney said, "but I'll tell you one thing, he's the finest."

"No."

"The finest."

"The colonel is."

"Not as a gunner. As a officer, yeah. Not as a gunner."

"Every way."

"No, no. Hell, man, just look at the scores."

"The scores ain't everything."

"Oh, yeah? What else is there?"

"They ain't everything."

They were going down the unlit stretch along the beach. The water was invisible, the color of the night. They rocked along like commuters, the axles squeaking. Cassada's head was bent down as if in thought, but his eyes were open. The light struck his cheekbones. Isbell was remembering, for no reason, the day he had come around the corner of the hangar with the flying suit wet and stuck to him and unwilling to go back and change. How for a moment, before knowing anything, Isbell had thought: this one's different.

"Listen," the sergeant said, "I was in Vegas close to three years. I seen them all."

"Oh, yeah? You remember the one took all the trophies at the meet there a couple of years back? That West Point major?"

"Sure. I know him. He's a real hotshot."

"What's his name again?"

"I know him," the sergeant said. "I seen him shoot."

"You think Lieutenant Piebes could beat him?"

"Hell, yes, he could."

"He ain't that good."

"You want to know what he told me about how he learned shooting?"

"What?"

"I was talking to him the other day and he said, Bonney, I learnt it from flying the tow ship."

"From what?"

"From flying the tow ship, he said."

"Hell, Bonney."

"No, that's right. That's right. It's like a caddie learns how to play golf." He looked around. "How do you think they learn? By watching good golfers, that's how."

He was searching for someone in the dark of the bus, squinting.

"Hey, Lieutenant," he said to Isbell. Then, moving his head a little, "What is it? Captain. I'm sorry. Listen, tell them, isn't that right, that the way to learn is to watch somebody doing it who really knows how?"

"That's one way."

"There you are," he cried.

"He ditn't say it was the best way."

"You heard the captain. I didn't say nothing about the best way. It don't have to be the best way. The best way is different for everybody, right, Captain?"

Isbell nodded.

Coming to the officers' area, the bus slowed down. When it stopped, Isbell and Cassada jumped off. The door groaned shut and like a battered metal curtain the side of the bus slid past them. They crossed towards their tent. Only the colonel's was noisy. Many people were asleep, ready for departure the next day. Off for Rome or Marseilles, the first leg home.

"What time do you plan to take off?" Cassada asked.

"Let's get going early. Right after breakfast."

"I hate to leave here," Cassada said.

"Maybe you picked up a thing or two."

"Sergeant Bonney. I don't know how much he really knows, but he wasn't that far off."

"It was a good week."

"This was the best thing that's happened to me since I've been in the squadron."

Two of Pine's pilots, Leeman and Sparrow, had taken off early and landed at Marseilles. Their planes were being refueled when Leeman came back from the metro office. Sparrow was waiting.

"All set? Are we ready to file?" he said.

Leeman was thin and known as the Deacon. He shook his head.

"Doesn't look like we're going anywhere today. The weather's down."

It was sunny and bright outside. Sparrow put down the paper.

"Come on," he said, "what is it, five thousand and five?"

"No, we're going to be here overnight."

"What do they have?"

"It's down to minimums. We might as well go into town."

Sparrow lifted his cap and smoothed his hair. His legs were stretched out in front of him. "Minimums," he said. Marseilles, though, was like that. Clear and fifteen and not another field open in Europe. Your only alternate is Marseilles—the countless times they heard that. "I'll be damned," he said. "Well, you know me."

"What do you mean?"

"I'm ready. Call a cab."

"We can go into Marignane," Leeman said. "They have a hotel there."

"Marignane?"

"It's not that far."

"Let's go to Marseilles."

"That's a long way."

"Come on, how much can it cost?"

"It's not that. I want to be able to get off first thing in the morning if the weather breaks up there."

"We can get up early."

"No."

"Oh, for God's sake. Why go anywhere? We can stay here and curl up right under the wing. That way we won't lose a minute."

"I don't want to drive all the way into Marseilles," Leeman told him.

They were still there in mid-afternoon waiting to see if the weather would change. Four more planes from Tripoli had landed and the pilots had gone into town. Leeman finally gave up.

"Let's go out and get our clothes bags," he said.

Another two ships were in the traffic pattern, just breaking and turning to downwind. It was Isbell's flight. They'd been delayed because of mechanical trouble. They landed and parked next to the planes already there.

"Must be weather," Isbell said to Cassada as they walked to operations.

Leeman and Sparrow were just leaving.

"What's the story?" Isbell said.

"Doesn't look good up there," Leeman told him. "I don't think you'll get home today."

"Where are you headed for?"

"We've got a taxi coming. We'll give you a ride if you want."

"I think we'll just have a look at things."

The French forecaster repeated what he had told the others. There was the influence of a deep low, he said, down to Lyons, on which city he tapped a knowing finger. Elbows on the counter, Isbell looked at the surface chart. There were no station sequences. The regular teletype net had been out since the day before, the forecaster said.

The big chart was twelve hours old, a forest of purple numbers and knotholes of pressure. There might be an alternate in England. Isbell felt a slight temptation. There were pilots who were apprehensive about weather and others for whom dense rain and fog were a lure, part of a reputation.

"Don't decide because of me," Cassada said. He was standing beside Isbell. "I can fly your wing through any of that."

Isbell felt the temptation.

"I'm with you, Captain."

"We'd have to penetrate, who knows, maybe from thirty thousand," Isbell said.

"I'll touch down right beside you."

There was the seductive image of the two of them, wheels folding birdlike beneath as they rose from the runway and headed north where no one else would go, where no one would dare to, but he was too wise to succumb to it. What was to be gained? Nothing useful.

"How much weather time do you have?" Isbell said.

"Actual weather?"

"Real weather, not under the hood."

"Twenty, twenty-five hours."

"Twenty-five?"

"Twenty. But the main thing is, how much do *you* have?"

Isbell looked at him. After a moment he acknowledged, "Plenty."

"Why don't we try it? We could always come back to Marseilles?"

"We can't file with Marseilles as an alternate. We'd have to find
something closer. I don't know if we can find anything."

"Couldn't we stretch the regulations a little?"

"No."

"Just to show these guys. Day, night, up, down, whatever, we do
it better."

For a moment Isbell saw them suddenly appearing beneath the
heavy, low clouds like couriers and taxiing in with somebody, Grace
maybe, maybe Dunning leaning out of the window of the Volksbus
and calling up. Isbell couldn't hear what they were saying. Chocks
were being put under the wheels. He took off his helmet and cupped
his ear.

"What?"

"We'd given up on you for today."

Isbell looked up at the ominous clouds just above his head that
represented the thing he was meant to avoid despite any pride: the
act that was indefensible, that proved nothing.

He looked at Cassada, the blue of his eyes, a pure undaunted blue.


"You suppose they're still out there?" Leeman asked.

Sparrow was pouring a beer. "What are you worried about?" he
said.

"I just don't want to be sitting around for nothing. I don't want
to have left Tripoli hours before them and get home a day later."

"Yeah. Humiliating."

"That's the trouble with you."

"What's wrong?" Sparrow said. "I do what I'm told. You say
Marignane—here we are. Captain Pine says log two hours every
flight, I log two hours. What am I supposed to do?"

"Never mind."

"I may not do everything on the dead run, but hey, the perfect wingman. I pad my flying time, I go to beer call, I know all the songs."

Leeman interrupted him with a slight, dampening motion of his hand.

"Why don't you have a beer?"

"Shut up a minute."

"What is it?"

"You hear that?"

Sparrow looked at the floor. He heard nothing. A car went by outside. "What?"

"That's them."

Sparrow listened again.

"It's somebody," he said. "It might not be them. It could be French."

"No."

"How can you tell?"

"I know. I know Isbell."

"Just by the sound of his engine? You're all right."

"That's them," Leeman repeated.

They listened. The sound rose a little, then faded.

"I'm going to call the field," Leeman said, "but that was them. I know it."

After a few minutes he came back, vindicated. He'd spoken to the forecaster who had finally come up with an alternate, Eindhoven. The weather there was at the edge of the low.

Ahead lay Valence, half in sunlight, half in shadow, grey against white with touches of gold. They were still climbing, passing twenty-five thousand. Off to the left was an autumn sun in the light of which Cassada's contrail gleamed, a late sun, emptied of heat. Long, clear rays. A sun that infused the canopy like crystal. Isbell could see the minute scratches in the plexiglas and in the rosy brown of his visor, unexpectedly, a huge eye, the size of a plum, his own. Moist pupil, dark watery iris, lashes. It was staring at something, unwary, intent. At itself.

He looked down toward the earth again and watched the line of the first clouds that, very low, divided Valence in two. Slowly all of it disappeared beneath the nose of the plane. The clouds were a vast glacier extending in all directions as far as he could see. Behind, like a departed shore, the last sight of the earth fell away. Brown hills were vanishing, a thin, polished river. Still in a climb they flew toward Lyons.

The clouds deepened as they went, the tops mounting. At thirty-five thousand Isbell leveled off. The tops were about twenty—it was difficult to say because they weren't solid though they looked it at first. There were large breaks in them. There were shaftways and passages. Milky rays of sunlight shot along them revealing caverns, abysses.

Nearing Lyons the needle of the radio compass began to waver. It fell off halfway, returned, then swung completely around. Isbell watched it, listening to the steady tone of the beacon and thinking not so much of the distance ahead but of how far they had come and how long a way it was back. The cockpit heat was not working well. His feet were cold and the top of the canopy had become white with little stars of frost, as exact as if they had been etched in the glass.

The sun fell lower. It was in the last quarter of its elevation, the light flat. The white of the clouds had faded like an old wall. Every-thing seemed silent and still as they headed towards Dijon. There was a strange, lost feeling, as though they were in an empty house, in rooms without furniture, looking through windows that had no glass. The world seemed abandoned. The last being had vanished from earth. There were ghostly cities below, desolate highways, meadows bathed in dead light. He had the map unfolded across his lap, looking ahead, listening to nothing. One lone sound reassured him, steady, unending, the sound of the engine, closer to him than breathing, more familiar than his heart.

As they swung Dijon, Isbell made a small x on the map, the point of his pencil going through. Beside it he wrote the time. A few minutes later he called Chaumont. He was already picking up their beacon.

There was no answer. After a pause, he called again. He was about to try a third time when he heard Cassada,

"They're answering you, Lead."

Cassada's transmission was weak. Isbell barely heard it.

"I can't read them," he said.

"White Lead from White Two," Cassada called.

"Go ahead."

"Chaumont Tower is calling you."

"Ask them for destination weather."

"Say again?"

Isbell was pressing the mike button harder, as if he could force his wingman to hear.

"The latest . . . destination . . . weather," he said very slowly. Chaumont was an American base, their weather information would be current.

"You want the latest weather?" There was something more that could not be made out.

"Roger."

"Say again?"

"Roger. The latest weather. The latest weather," Isbell said.

He could hear Cassada transmitting but not clearly. There was a long silence. He began to be uneasy. It was hard to wait. They were traveling seven or eight miles each minute. The sun had sunk lower and a different cast was coming over the sky. In the distance, purples were appearing, the last faint reds. He looked to the east. There, past Italy, were the pillars of night, the deep, welling blues following in the wake of the sun, crossing the invisible Alps, darkening tidelike the clouds of Salzburg, Munich.

"Did you get that?" he heard.

"Negative."

"Did you get the weather, Lead?"

"Negative, negative," Isbell said.

"I can't read you. It's five hundred overcast and two miles. . . ." There was something else, unintelligible.

"What do they have at Chaumont?"

"I can't read you at all. You're very weak and garbled."

Isbell repeated his transmission four or five times. Finally he was understood. He waited. They were past Chaumont by then. The sun was just above the top deck of clouds. The quiet was unnerving. There was an immense, long silence. Time slowed. The minutes grew.

Isbell heard nothing more. His radio was dead, there was not even a side tone. He switched from one channel to another, trying to call or hear anybody. There was nothing. *Five hundred and two,* he was thinking, trying to consider it calmly. The sun was just touching the clouds, tangent to the highest layer, turning it dark as if an act were ending. They had been flying more than an hour. *Five hundred and two.*

He looked out at Cassada and began rocking his wings. He looked at the map. It was more than four hundred miles back to Marseilles. Cassada hadn't moved. Isbell rocked his wings again. Cassada banked gently in towards him. He watched him curve in slowly, the white wake bending, and slide perfectly to Isbell's wingtip.

Isbell passed a hand in front of his face two or three times and touched the side of his helmet. He saw Cassada nod. He tapped his oxygen mask. Another nod. Transmitter and receiver both out. He was still turning things over in his mind. They were only ten or fifteen minutes out. He could feel Cassada waiting, watching, wondering perhaps, though able to talk to the ground. *I'm going to touch down right beside you.* It would be the reverse. Finally Isbell pointed a finger at him, then pointed straight ahead. Cassada's ship moved forward.

Isbell was now flying wing. In the silence he hung there. All that remained in the world was the other airplane. He stared at it. Every detail was terrifically clear. He read the black numbers on the tail. He watched the other plane move, rising slightly, sinking, as if borne by the calmest sea. It seemed incredibly heavy against the sky. He watched Cassada's head move, nod—he was talking to someone— then look this way and that. What was he saying? What were they

telling him? Isbell began switching channels again, fumbling
blindly for the set which was behind his left elbow. He called on
each frequency, aching to hear something. He saw then that they
had started to descend. He glanced at the clouds beneath. They were
dark, profound.

They were at twenty thousand, the station still ahead. A thousand years had passed since Marseilles. Isbell glanced quickly at the
needle. It was steady. They were close. It was holding dead on as if
anchored. When he looked again it had begun to waver, darting
from side to side. Speed brakes, he thought, and almost at that
moment saw Cassada give the hand signal. In unison they put them
out. The noses pitched down. The attitude steepened.

At twelve thousand feet they began the turn to come back
inbound. The cloud tops were streaming just beneath them, the
threatening grey domes. Cassada's wingtip lights came on. Isbell
reached for his own, the panel lights also. Ten thousand feet. In a
bank. The clouds were skimming below. In a silence that existed for
Isbell alone they went down together towards the hidden earth.

† † † † † † † † † †

They were racing through densities, uneven, unending. One minute Cassada's plane was clear, iron-hard in the gloom, and the next almost gone except for the wingtip light. When Isbell rode a little high he could see the red glow in the other cockpit, the aura of the instruments and even their circular faces, Cassada's head bent forward towards them, motionless, intent. It was dusk in the clouds. It was deep rain-grey.

They broke out low the first time and off to the side. Isbell had one real look. Cassada saw it himself and they began turning, banking steeply across the runway at about two hundred feet and then reversing, cutting back hard. Isbell wasn't sure what they were doing, if Cassada meant to try and put it down there with half of the runway or even more behind them. He felt a moment of panic and suddenly saw Cassada was pulling away from him. Speed brakes in. He had missed the signal. Perhaps it hadn't been given. He caught up using full power just as Cassada held out a fist with thumb extended: gear up. Then flaps. They were climbing, into the overcast again, turning north.

Isbell was sweating. His legs felt light, the knees missing. Don't watch the fuel, he said to himself, don't look at it. He kept trying the mike button, not in desperation but there might be a loose connection somewhere, it might kick in again. He talked but no sound came, his voice was dead in the oxygen mask, trapped in it. His right hand, on the stick, kept tightening. He had to think to make it relax. Don't look, he told himself. Forget it. It hasn't changed. It hasn't even been a minute. All right. Robert, don't be in a hurry now. Don't get excited. It's a little bad maybe, but just do it right. Set it up this time. Make it perfect. Don't be in a rush. Everything in order. Everything so.

They had leveled at twenty-five hundred feet, still heading north. Isbell was following things by glances at his own instruments. He sat waiting for the turn. His mind was racing ahead. He was trying to think, trying to stem the anguish, force the runway to appear dead ahead with them settling in towards it together, whistling, fast, and the sudden jar of the wheels hitting.

Cassada still hadn't turned. Isbell stole a look at the clock. It meant nothing. Finally, when he felt he could not bear it another second, he realized they were banking. The unseen world was tilting, heeling over on a blind axis. They were talking to Cassada, he knew. They were telling him things, giving him numbers more precious than safe combinations. Every so often his head would nod a little.

The downwind was interminable. At last they turned onto base leg, the gear coming down with its faint, assuring quake. The last preparations. Isbell pushed back in the seat, sitting straighter. A glance at the fuel. One warranted look. Nine hundred pounds. He could feel his heart starting in.

All right, Robert, he said. Now exactly the way they give it to you. Easy, smooth, not paying attention to anything else, just as if it were clear as a bell here, as if it were only practice.

# V

FINALLY CASSADA ANSWERS . . .

Finally Cassada answers. He's on top at nine thousand, orbiting the beacon. Dunning doesn't need to ask but can't prevent himself,

"Do you have White Two up there?"

"Negative. I can't see him anywhere."

"How's your fuel?"

"I've got five hundred pounds," Cassada replies. It's like a heavy door closing.

"Look around. Can't you spot him?"

A pause.

"You'd better get him down," Cadin says.

Godchaux steps out of the doorway and his eyes meet Harlan's. They each know what the other is thinking.

After a few moments the controller comes on just as Cassada says something, and the transmissions block each other out. It's brief but it seems to introduce something, an unwanted confusion. Either no one is talking or they all are.

"Do you have White Two?" Cassada asks the controller.

"Roger," the controller says.

"Where is he? What's his position?"

"Four miles northeast. Heading inbound."

"What altitude?" Dunning breaks in.

"You were blocked, White," the controller says.

"What's his altitude?"

"Who am I talking to?"

"Mobile Control."

". . . together?" It's the last part of something Cassada is asking.

"Take up a heading of three three zero," the controller instructs.

"What's his altitude?" Dunning is shouting. "What's White Two's altitude?"

"Stand by one," the controller says.

It seems minutes pass. Dunning pulls out a handkerchief to wipe his nose and jams it back in his pocket, the tip hanging out. Then Cassada's voice says,

"This gauge is jumping around."

No one answers him. There is no answer.

"It just dropped," he says. "It's down to three hundred pounds."

His voice has a lost quality. No one replies.

"Now it's going back and forth between three and five hundred."

"White Lead?" the controller says, unable to address the matter of fuel.

"Roger."

"White Two is three miles out," the controller reports. Then, "He's holding level at fifteen hundred feet." It means in the densest clouds.

"Say again his altitude," Dunning calls.

"White Two is at one thousand five hundred."

There's a silence.

"Did you receive that, White Lead?"

"Roger."

"What are your intentions?"

He doesn't answer. He had climbed up, low on fuel, in a last attempt to find his leader. Should he abandon him now? Was it too late?

Dunning, stripped of hope like someone who has just lost all his money, everything, but unwilling to show it with the colonel beside him, stands with the microphone in one hand, a microphone that is useless. Abruptly coming to life again, he says,

"Come on down, Cassada. You can make it. The runway lights are showing up good now. You'll spot them this time." His eyes sweep the length of things outside. "Come on, boy. Penetrate right from where you are."

"Roger."

"How much fuel do you have?"

"Three hundred pounds. I can't tell. It's jumping around."

"You can make it," Dunning says. You can make it, you can make it, he says to himself.

✝ ✝ ✝ ✝ ✝ ✝ ✝ ✝ ✝ ✝

Get us on, Isbell was thinking, get us on. They were trying the third time but everything was running the wrong way, he could feel it, a tide in the dark pulling at his legs. Get us on. He was either saying or thinking it when suddenly they came skimming out of the clouds in the moment of revelation, his heart rising up into his throat.

This time he saw it all. They had come down even lower, a hundred feet off the ground, bursting in and out of the ragged scud. Instants of vision, then into it again. The runway, the yellow mobile, everything passing by on the left as he saw it was like the others, no good. There welled up in him without thinking, oh, God, and looking down for a second too long he was late as Cassada turned. He turned hard himself, following, watching the ship ahead, the ground, clouds, the control tower almost straight on. Then Cassada was gone into a cloud lower than the rest. Isbell was in trail. He would see Cassada on the other side in a moment. Two moments. Longer. The cloud did not end. They never emerged. Isbell was on his own instruments, climbing. The tops were far above. The bases were frightening. He was climbing alone.

He was unable to think. He didn't know what heading he was on. It meant nothing just then. He was watching the fuel gauge. They were sometimes off by a couple hundred pounds. On top, he was thinking, on top. He could not concentrate on anything but that. The brightness above. To circle for a moment there within sight of the sky. He did not know whether there was something else he might be doing or not. He had to climb.

It became a little easier the higher he went. The airplane was flying as if it could go on forever. It was powerful, light. He didn't wonder about Cassada, where he had gone. There was nothing left but a silent, darkening world, rock-hard, waiting for him to fall. He looked again at the fuel gauge. He was unable to keep his eyes from it, no matter how hard he tried.

Harlan stands with Godchaux near the doorway. All of them are listening. The controller reports Isbell two miles out, and he's switching to guard channel, the emergency channel, in case Isbell can receive—as if he *is* receiving—giving him corrections. There's no response to them. As if flown by a dead man, Isbell's plane is coming straight in.

The GCA van, beside the runway, has no windows. The plane may come right out of the clouds, directly at it or towards mobile.

"Get ready to move out of here in a hurry," Harlan says in a low voice to Godchaux.

"What'd you say?"

Harlan repeats it.

"Don't worry," Godchaux whispers.

They have Isbell a mile and a half out. The rain is still falling, like drops of ice. Harlan stands close to the side of mobile, partly sheltered, listening. The visibility is worse, if anything. He looks at Godchaux.

He ain't going to get down, Harlan thinks. If he does, they'll go crazy. They'll make a big hero out of him and we'll never get done hearing about it. Not that he will, but things are funny sometimes. You never know.

One mile now. Dunning ducks a little, looking all around. He turns the volume down slightly to listen. Godchaux touches Harlan on the arm.

"What?" Then Harlan hears it himself. He nods.

It's Isbell for certain. They barely hear him. They stand there peering into the rain. The sound gets no louder.

"Major," Godchaux says.

Dunning quickly comes to the door, Cadin behind him.

"Do you hear him?" Dunning says.

"I think so."

Suddenly the sound is closer, unmistakable. It comes beating, like waves.

"That's him!" Dunning agrees.

They stare in the direction of the sound but see nothing. It feels as if he's headed straight for them.

"Where is he?" Dunning asks. He has the flare gun in his hand and holds it outside the door. The sound is becoming louder, rushing at them like a roof collapsing. There's a sudden explosion as Dunning shoots off a green flare.

"Do you have him?" he shouts.

"There he is!"

Almost straight up with a roar as it passes overhead, almost on top of them. Black gear wells, a great smooth belly, and then it's past. For a second the sound doesn't fade, it even increases and then begins to fall away, faster than it came. Harlan is shaking a little, he can't help it.

"Shit," Dunning says.

Then, despite the low volume, Cassada is calling. They have him on downwind. Dunning seems not even to hear. He stares out the glass towards where Isbell moments before has disappeared. Cassada is turning onto base. He's down to two hundred pounds.

In his mind Isbell prepares it. The details merge, become entangled. He forces his way through them, striving to make them distinct. He watches the instruments as he climbs, it seems to take a minute to read each one. A hundred and fifty pounds. He has made the decision but cannot move. He sits frozen, trying to believe.

Twenty-five hundred feet. He is delaying but can't think why. At any moment there'll be a surge, the gauges dying then coming back. The expectation makes him hollow. His hand won't move. He looks down at the red handle that blows the canopy. He can't touch it. The first, warning lurch will make him jump like a cat but he does nothing. The engine is steady, the plane intact.

One hundred pounds. The agony of the end. With an abrupt movement he levels the wings. He was rolling into a bank unaware. Pull it now, he thinks. Then sit erect. Squeeze the forked handles. He knows it from a thousand recitations. Pull. He can't.

The safety pin. Suddenly he thinks of that and looks down. It's out. Three thousand feet. Should he begin slowing? The clouds are a death shroud. He is climbing for the last time, sick, clinging to a dream that is over. The cockpit lights gleam in the glass above his head. Fifty pounds. He levels off and reduces power. He feels nothing. He is a ghost who is flying. Then in an instant that passes. He thinks: I have to do it now. I have to move my hands.

He tries. They glide across his lap, independent, light. The left takes the stick. The right drops down and takes hold of the handle, round in his palm. He tightens his fingers and gathers himself. Ready. Pull!

Nothing happens. His hand will not do it. It's like trying to pull out a tooth. Mechanically, like a child, he starts counting. One . . . two . . . The next word jams. He begins again, resolute. One . . . Two . . . A pause. Three! He yanks up. The air explodes, icy, vast. The canopy is gone. A roaring surrounds him. He almost feels regret. Scraps of paper flash by. The maps inflate, rise past him and are torn away. The wind is tearing at his clothes. I've done it, he thinks! The relief is so great he could laugh.

Suddenly he feels a heave. The ship hesitates for a moment and goes forward again. He can't make out the instruments. It doesn't matter. He could smash them with a hammer, break everything. All is profaned, all is going and at any moment, a terminal sounding, fierce and ultimate. The death dive. Get out, he thinks. He realizes he can't tell what attitude it's taking. He might be rolling over, blind, out of control. Get out!

He sits there trying to think. He has hold of the forked ejection grip and is beginning to squeeze when there's another hesitation, mortal, abrupt. A surge as the engine catches again. The last of the fuel. He forces his head back against the heavy plate, tenses his legs bringing them close, and before he knows what has happened, with a shock, a hunching jolt, his fist holding the two leaves tight together, he is gone, through the darkness, into the black air.

The rain is falling steadily now. "Zero six four, White," the controller is saying. "You're five and a half miles out."

Harlan and Godchaux are crowded into the doorway. The runway lights are bright in the darkness.

"Zero six four," the controller repeats.

"Here, load this again." Dunning hands Godchaux the flare gun.

From the cardboard box of cartridges Godchaux takes several and tries to read the printing on their base.

"A green one," Dunning says.

"Yes, sir."

Harlan lights a match and holds it so they can see.

"Your final cockpit check should be complete. Your gear should be down and locked. Zero six four," the controller says.

The fire trucks are parked together halfway down, their red lights flashing and swinging around.

"Stand there, Billy. Fire it when he's close enough," Dunning orders.

Godchaux is searching for a second green shell.

Bail out, Dunning should be ordering but can't bring himself to say it. Perhaps Cadin will. If just one of them gets down. Isbell's they can probably get away with. Materiel failure, the radio. The board will buy that.

"Zero six four is your heading, bringing you in nicely towards the center line. Glide path coming up in ten seconds. Zero six four."

Ten seconds. His last call was two hundred pounds, Dunning thinks. He's down to fifty by now, waiting for it to flame out, to drop from under him. He should be bailing out. Why wasn't he told to, they'll want to know? Because we thought he could make it, is all Dunning can think. After he missed three attempts? There must be an answer to that.

"Left three degrees to zero six one."

Dunning appears calm.

"Begin your rate of descent."

Supervisory error, they will say. No, he wasn't told to bail out. I felt he had a good chance.

"Zero six one has you lined up tracking the right side of the runway. Zero six one."

They are all peering outside into the slanting rain.

"Dropping slightly low on the glide path, White," the controller announces. "Ten feet. Twenty feet."

"Get ready, Billy."

"Right." Godchaux goes down a couple of steps.

"Coming back now, correcting nicely. Ten feet low. Back on glide path again. Left to zero six zero."

If he lands, when he climbs down from the cockpit his legs will be shaking like leaves, his face will be white. If he lands he will be unable to speak.

The telephone rings. Harlan picks it up.

"Dropping slightly low, White."

"It's for you, Major."

"Ten, twenty feet low."

"Tell them to hold on."

"You're dropping forty feet low, White."

Dunning's heart skips.

"Get ready, Billy. He may break out any second."

"Seventy-five."

"Jesus Christ."

"He'd better bail out. Tell him to bail out," Cadin says.

"Bail out, White!" Dunning calls.

"A hundred feet. You're dangerously low. You're dropping into our ground clutter, White. Pull it up!"

"Bail out, White! Bail out, do you hear me?"

There is silence.

"Fortify White," the controller says, "execute a missed approach. Climb straight ahead to twenty-five hundred feet."

There is no answer.

"Fortify White, acknowledge, please."

"Pull it up, White, and get out!"

"Fortify White," the controller calls, "Fortify White."

"White from mobile! Pull up and eject. Do you read?"

There's a long pause. It's quiet. The silence is now rising like water, deep, deeper.

"Did you hear anything?" Dunning asks Godchaux.

Godchaux shakes his head and comes inside, the flare gun dangling from his hand. The controller continues to talk, the same things over and over, like a telephone ringing somewhere. Everything else is still, the air, the lights, the nearly silent rain. Harlan holds out the telephone receiver. Dunning takes it.

"Major Dunning," he says.

No one is there. There are voices in the background.

"Hello! Major Dunning here!"

Someone picks up the phone and says, "Stand by for a second, please." It must be the tower.

The fire trucks are backing up and turning around, heading away from the runway. Dunning hangs up the phone.

"Let's go," Cadin says. "We'll take my car."

At the bottom of the steps his foot slips on the wet grass and he goes down on one knee, stands again and makes it to the car.

Godchaux and Harlan follow in the Volksbus, bouncing over the turf. They turn onto the taxiway and head for the squadron gate. The window of Dunning's office is still open and the lights on as they pass. Below, on the road past the airmen's barracks, the fire trucks, alarmingly lit, are speeding.

The year before, at Landstuhl, they had one where half the base was out searching and they didn't find the pilot for two days. Of course, that was in thick fog, you couldn't see ten feet.

Both of them, Dunning thinks as they drive. Jesus Christ. They slow down at the gate. The guard steps out of the shack, bending over to see.

"Emergency. Plane crash," Cadin says, rolling down the window.

"Yes, sir." He waves them through.

On the way, thinking of the one at Landstuhl, "We might have to organize search parties," Dunning says.

"Let's see what we've got, first," the colonel says.

About a mile down the road are the fire trucks, blocking it. There's also an ambulance with headlights on. The rain, now white, floats through the beams shining like bits of tinfoil.

"Which way is it?" Cadin asks a figure standing there. A flashlight is swung and shines in his face. "Turn that goddamn thing off," he says.

The beam flicks to his shoulder for a second and then goes out.

"Sorry, sir." It's one of the firemen. There are voices out in the darkness shouting to one another.

"Have they found the pilot?"

"Sir, I don't know. It's straight ahead, about a quarter of a mile. I've been here with the truck."

"Let me borrow your flashlight," Cadin says, taking it from him. He and Dunning get out and begin to walk, first along the road and then off, in the direction of some handheld lights. The ground is soft and gives underfoot. The rain sweeps down. From time to time, moving in silence, they break into a trot. Godchaux and Harlan come behind.

Ahead is a small pond and beyond it blackness. There are wandering lights and soon the first pieces on the ground.

"Here's something," Godchaux calls.

He picks it up. Cadin's flashlight plays on it. Impossible to say what it is. A metal shard. Perhaps part of a hydraulic cylinder—it has a sticky sheen.

A trail of debris begins. There is ammunition scattered on the ground, some of it linked together, the rest strewn like teeth. Then a large piece, one of the gun bay panels. The drop tanks. Cadin stands, moving the beam back and forth over a large section of wing. Harlan kicks at something, stoops and picks it up gingerly.

"Shine it this way, Colonel."

The first ominous chord. It's a shoe. Harlan holds it slightly away from himself and turns it so he can see inside.

"It's empty."

He places it alongside his own foot. It's smaller.

Twenty feet farther on there is something pale floating in a small puddle. Godchaux reaches down. The water is deeper than it looks. He pulls up a map, soggy and dripping, a course drawn on it in grease pencil. There are other scraps of paper around, pages from the maintenance forms. At the edge of some woods they come to the end of it. The emblem of disaster, the engine, huge, with dirt packed into it, is at the base of a tree, the trunk marked with a great, white gouge.

They stand, looking over the scene.

"I don't see the seat anywhere," Dunning says.

"No."

It may be elsewhere, part of an ejection.

"We ought to work back."

"Yes," the colonel agrees. "Spread out more."

Feet soaked, they walk through the rain, moving slowly. Ahead are two or three lights jerking from spot to spot on the ground. The sky is invisible, absolutely black. It's like being in a mine or a deep, underground cave. They stumble over rocks. Then Harlan calls,

"Over here!"

The flashlight glides to something, hard to make out.

"Here's the cockpit," Harlan says.

The flashlight stays on it, then other lights as searchers converge. The seat is lying on its side, ripped free. It's empty. Cadin's light moves to a section of the instrument panel and picks out the black gauges. Harlan is bending over something a few feet away.

"What is it?"

"Canopy frame," he says.

They look at the seat again. The safety belt is unbuckled. Dunning tries to calculate what that might mean. The ejection handle hasn't been raised. The seat wasn't fired.

"That's where we found him," somebody says.

Cadin's light comes up and holds there. It's a corpsman, white uniform visible beneath a raincoat. He wears a pair of rubber boots.

"Dead?" Cadin says.

The corpsman nods. "Yes, sir."

The cold is making them shiver. Rain runs down their faces. Dunning has borrowed a flashlight and goes off by himself, poking his way from piece to piece, making small, slow circles at his feet with the light. He stops and then goes on, aimlessly it seems. He is gathering the catastrophe, wandering in it like a sleepwalker. The wreckage is total. Nothing can recombine it.

"Do you suppose he blacked out or something, Lieutenant?" the corpsman asks Godchaux who lingers behind.

"Do I suppose what?"

"Blacked out. You know."

"No. He ran out of fuel."

"Oh," the corpsman says, nodding. He turns half away. "It really broke up, didn't it?" He turns back to Godchaux, the beads of water shining on his raincoat and running off. "It doesn't look like they'll be putting this one back together again, does it?"

"Sure," Godchaux says. "They'll have it flying again inside of a week."

He walks towards the major, shaking his head.

† † † † † † † † † † †

No sound except for the clock. Beyond the windows the night is fading, smooth from the passage of hours. Exhausted from the same dream over and over, Isbell wakes. His eyes see nothing. It's silent and cold. He lies in bed aching, too ancient to move. Out there somewhere, more silent still, in the matted grass the wreckages lie, blown apart in the darkness, wet as the ground. They are miles from each other yet they are one. The earth is soft from the rain. The marks of tires in it are blurring, the print of feet. The photographers have yet to come. A mournful stillness covers it all.

He looks toward the windows. It's close to daybreak. The paleness of dawn. He is writing his statement again, sitting at a desk in base operations, the one survivor, strong but shaken, putting it down while it's fresh. The pen feels like a stick in his fingers. He writes automatically, as if copying something. What he is writing he doesn't know. They are walking in and out almost aimlessly, back from the scene. Their shoes are muddy. He can hear the talking plainly. Occasionally he is asked a question. The flight surgeon has gone off to get some sleeping pills though Isbell has said he doesn't need any. "You might." Isbell is too tired to argue.

Dunning's hand is there on his shoulder. The hand is consoling, but it's impossible to write with it there. After a while Dunning walks away and Isbell resumes, adding one sentence to another. It seems endless. It requires so much time. He is listening, writing, and thinking all at once. The overheard words beat in on him strangely. He's far off, thinking of different things entirely, drawn into a kind of dream of what it was like six hours, a day, a month before. A time of innocence. He longs for it like a murderer. He yearns for the past. Around him they are discussing it in lowered voices. He knows how long it will go on, turning into testimony, transcripts, findings. The board will meet, the attached documents mount up. That there should begin the long, careful process of determining exactly what caused the accident is right, but it will only reveal the facts. He could almost save them the trouble. He could put it all in a single phrase, but it would be too incomprehensible, too derelict. Somewhere within him there was, there could still be, a flaw. It could never have occurred otherwise.

He sits on the edge of the bed, then stands by the window. The low clouds are still there. He can make them out, smooth as a river. The sky is close to the earth, just beginning to appear. Beneath his naked feet the floor is cold. He stands shivering, alone. The reaction is always delayed, the shaking. His knee hurts. He had somehow twisted it, it feels stiff and unbending.

"What's wrong?"

Marian's voice is husky. She is up on one elbow. In the half-light her face is soft and wondering, like a child's. The dark hair around it is pressed by sleep.

"What are you doing? Are you all right?"

"Nothing. I'm just thinking."

She takes a deep, sympathetic breath. "Can't you sleep?"

He wants to embrace her instead of answering, the look of her, the loyalty. At that moment she seems everything in life.

In Puerto Rico, sighing at midnight, they are aware of nothing. Cassada's mother is sleeping, his cousins and friends. He still exists there, this last night. He shines in their sleep like an exploded star, the son who was killed in Germany in a flying accident, the only son.

"Try and sleep," Marian murmurs and falls back to the bed, rolling onto her side and hitting at the pillow once or twice to make it right. In a minute she is gone.

He is left thinking. The events of the evening before, as distinct as when they were happening, loom up like a wall and repeat themselves over and over. He tries to change them but they are unalterable. He tries to think of something else. We parted without a word. There were many things he'd intended to say, that he might have said, given time. Now that it is too late he is certain that Cassada bore something unique, something they had missed, the sum of their destinies. It was true Isbell had sometimes opposed him. It had been essential to. It was part of the unfolding.

The clouds are heavy in the dawn. Beneath, the world is in shadow. Above, there is sunlight, unseen. Beyond, the invisible stars. Cassada, too, had been unable to say certain things. He hadn't the power to. All that was to come.

"To die is to sink from the sight of this world," the chaplain intones, voice filling the quiet. "It is to sink from the sight of this world and to rise again in God."

The air is stuffy, as if the windows have not been opened in a long time. Isbell and his wife are in the first row, along with the Dunnings. Wickenden sits two rows behind and Harlan a row behind that, next to the aisle, worrying something out of his back teeth with his tongue.

"It is to attain Christ," the chaplain says, "to be reborn to life, to enter into pure light. We think of this young officer and involuntarily we exclaim: how short, how brief a life. In the midst, in the very fullness of it, he is gone."

Someone, a woman, gives a short, quavering sigh.

"And still," says the chaplain, "what an example he affords. To give one's life in the service of your country. To die a hero's death. It's a story we cannot hear without wonder and admiration. A short life, yes, but the number of years in itself is nothing, nor is it given to us to know when God will call us or what circumstances He will elect."

The order was, everyone in a blouse. With ribbons. Wickenden had decided to wear only the Victory Medal but changed his mind at the last minute and was wearing nothing but the Purple Heart.

"That the only one you have?" Dunning asked.

"It's the only one I value, Major," Wickenden said.

Bored, Wickenden glances at the windows, high up in the wall. Only the bottoms of them are stained; the tops are clear glass. Through them bright sky can be seen, sunlight coming down between the clouds in dazzling, thick columns. A perfect day for flying. And here we sit, he thinks.

"I remember the very day," the chaplain is saying, "as I am sure you do. I remember how grey and dreary it was, ending in rain, and as I do, I think of him trying to come home through it, to return safe to port, as it were, after a hazardous voyage. I think of him as he strove through darkness seeking to fulfill his mission, to land his airplane while heroically guiding another pilot, his leader, who would have been lost without him."

Wickenden feels scorn. His wife is looking down at her shoes. He was right, he was right all along. That can be a bad thing, but at the moment it doesn't matter. He feels only the satisfaction of it, of having been redeemed. Phil, his wife, turns her head a little and for a moment they look into each other's eyes. Then she withdraws. She is not that unpitying or cold. She lifts her head and watches the chaplain.

He's pouring it on, Wickenden thinks in disgust. I always thought the Catholics didn't have any sermons. Don't know what gave me that idea. They have them, all right. They can hold their own with any of them.

"That he failed to save himself," says the chaplain, "seems to me a measure of the man. That he sought to save another, there is the answer and the mark of his worthiness. He rose to the challenge. Is there greater praise? It may not be given to many of us to be tested as Lieutenant Cassada was—the Lord decides—but it is given to us to strive, as he did, through the darkness and to seek salvation.

"What he did succeed in doing was to give us an example of courage and duty we will never forget. I ask you now to pray for him with me. He may not be beyond the help of prayer."

Isbell, subdued though not by anything he is hearing, is thinking of what he would give to have it not have happened. He is almost sickened by it, the guilt. Cassada himself stands before him, fairhaired, his small mouth and teeth, young, unbeholden. There was an elegance about him, a superiority. You did not find it often.

Behind him someone is sobbing. Someone blows their nose. *Striving through darkness*—among the few words he will remember. That much at least is true.

It was his beauty, of course, a beauty that no one saw—they were blind to such a thing—except perhaps for Ferguson who was an outsider himself, but even Mayann Dunning with her acute sensitivity to the masculine missed it. By beauty, nothing obvious is meant. It was an aspect of the unquenchable, of the martyr, but this quality had its physical accompaniment. His shoulders were luminous, his body male but not hard, his hair disobedient. Few of them had seen him naked, not that he concealed himself or was modest but like some animal come to drink he was solitary and unboisterous. He was intelligent but not cerebral and could be worshipful, as in the case of airplanes. He would be remembered not as the chaplain described him but in certain recollections, someone seen and not forgotten like the god who raised his hand at the farmboys, filling their meager hearts.

At length it was over. Everyone stood. Isbell saw it was Jackie Grace behind them. She sat, tears running down her cheeks, people pretending not to look at her. Up the aisle they walk, heads bowed.

Among the women tears could begin by just one of them starting to cry. In the vestibule Grace is waiting for his wife. He shrugs a little, helplessly, as Godchaux passes.

On the sidewalk outside they stand gathered, the women holding their hats on in the wind. As the last people come through the doors there is the sound of planes and they look up. Two flights of four in trail. Only seven ships however. The number three position in the first flight is empty. Directly overhead they come across the chapel, covering it with noise. The chaplain hurries out to look, but too late. They're gone. The deep noise is borne off by the wind. Good-bye, Isbell thinks. Something pulls at his heart. The chaplain is looking around as if the planes might come back, as if he has merely missed the opening act.

Wickenden's wife is digging in her pocketbook for a handkerchief. "I can't help it," she says, touching her eyes. "It's that missing one. It always makes me sad."

"One of the few real things left," Wickenden says.

"Every time I see it. I can't help it."

"At least they were right on time," he says. "They looked pretty good."

"I still think you should do it, his own squadron."

"Who'd go to the services then? The 72nd?"

"I guess it can't be that way," she says, bowing again to his logic.

"It's a good idea, but I don't think they'd buy it."

Eyes red, trying to smile, Jackie Grace wanders about. Every time another woman takes her hand she breaks into tears.

"Poor Jackie," Wickenden's wife says.

"Hard to understand."

"What do you mean?"

"Imagine what she'd be like if it was Grace we were burying."

"Oh, you are a hard man."

As they are getting ready to drive off, Dumfries comes up and taps on the window. Wickenden rolls it down.

"Captain, are we supposed to go back to the squadron this afternoon?"

"I haven't heard any different. Have you?"

"No, sir. I thought I'd better ask."

"What do you want to do, go play with Laurie?"

"Sir?"

"Forget it. What I meant to say was, regardless of what the chaplain said I don't think they've made this a national holiday yet."

"We have to go back, then?"

"Yes."

"Oh. That's what I thought."

A moment later he returns.

"I'll be out of your way in just a minute," he says, pointing to his car which is wedged in close to theirs.

"Good."

He smiles and waves a little as he trots off. His wife, looking demure as a bridesmaid, is waiting for him to unlock the door for her. She turns towards the Wickendens' car and smiles, too.

Dumfries pulls out with Wickenden right behind him. The speed limit is fifteen miles an hour which he dutifully observes. The road curves around the commissary and up a small hill. At the top the rolling landscape and valleys are visible. The chapel below is in sunlight, a few people still standing outside the door.

"Well, they should have listened to you."

"Sometimes you wonder why you even bother," Wickenden says. "You can't reason with people. It's a waste of time."

"They should have listened to you."

"They know everything already."

"But who was really in a better position to know?"

"They think *I'm* pigheaded."

"Maybe after this they'll listen."

"Because it turned out I was right?"

"Yes."

"I doubt it. Usually it works out just the opposite."

"It's really a shame."

"The accident?"

"That you're not in charge."

"I know."

A glass in one hand, Mayann regards herself in the mirror, turns slightly one way, then the other, puts the glass down on the night table, and somewhat too deliberately smooths her dress around the hips where it looked a little tight. She looks for the cigarette she had a minute ago, but it isn't there. It's in the bathroom or living room or both. She has a sip of the drink and closer to the mirror examines her eyes. Still young. Young enough. She takes a deep, nostalgic breath. For some reason she thinks of driving, being driven, leaning back in the seat, the road pouring by. The night wind, the radio on. A little cool jazz. All those times, she thinks. There is the sound of a key in the lock and the door closing.

"Bud?"

"Damn cold out," Dunning says, coming down the hallway. "It's winter again."

He stands in the doorway. Mayann nods at her glass.

"Want to join me?"

"What have you been doing, having a little party?"

"Having a drink."

"*A* drink."

"I may have another."

"That's a surprise."

"You've never had a drink?"

He looks at her and looks away.

"Well, how'd it go?" she says. "Kill anyone else today?"

"What in the hell's wrong with you?"

"Nothing."

"I don't know about that."

"Forget what I said."

"I don't consider that funny. Neither should you. I see you didn't bother to change your dress."

"So? You didn't change your uniform."

"I work in my uniform."

"You work wearing all your medals?"

"You wear them sometimes. What are you getting at? I gave the order to wear them. Wickenden didn't bother to obey it."

"Seems like you have more of them than you used to. Can that be? You don't have any duplicates in there, do you?"

"Just what's bothering you?"

"What's that one again?" she says, pointing.

"What's what one?"

"Purple Heart, right?"

"Stop it."

"Don't get angry. I just forget what they all are. God, there's enough of them. Little bronze doodads. You must have more than anybody. You earned them, I know."

"Each and every one of them."

"I'm just happy to see you haven't lost any, misplaced them somewhere. I mean, they're very small. Compared to other things."

"Now what does that mean?"

"That's for me to know, isn't it?"

"I don't know if you really know anything. You don't act like it. Is there any beer in the refrigerator?"

"Search me."

"Thanks."

"You don't have to thank me. Search me, that's all. I don't know."

Dunning goes to find a beer, opens it, and comes out of the kitchen cleaning the lip of the bottle with his palm. He sits down with the newspaper. For a minute or so he reads in silence.

"Didn't that sicken you a little today?" Mayann asks.

There is a soft sound as Dunning, not answering, turns the page.

"What?" he finally says.

"Didn't that make you a little sick today?"

"Didn't what make me sick?"

"That sermon. All that stuff. Doesn't anybody tell these chaplains what's really going on?"

Dunning takes a swallow of beer and sets the bottle down again. He turns another page and unbuttons his blouse. His shirt is tight over his belly. From across the room his wife looks at him, big legs stretched out in front of him.

"Why doesn't somebody clue them in?" she says.

"Fine. Why don't you?"

"I'm hardly the one to do that."

"You can say that again," Dunning says.

"You bastard."

"Watch yourself. Enough's enough, you know what I mean?"

"It was so phony. That wasn't the way it happened."

"It was something like that," Dunning said wearily.

"It wasn't right," she insisted. "It was just words."

"Maybe you'd like to be the chaplain."

"No, I want you to answer me."

"Answer you what?"

"You know what I mean. Don't you feel it?"

"I've got a lot more to worry about than the chaplain." He lowers the newspaper. "In case you don't know it, I might get relieved. I might lose the squadron."

Mayann is silent but feels a chill. Although she doesn't care about the Officers' Wives Club, she knows she is in a position not to care. They have to respect her, but not if she weren't a squadron commander's wife, if her husband was only another major.

"It wasn't your fault."

"Tell 'em that."

"It wouldn't be fair."

He raises the paper again and mutters a single word,

"Shit."

After a few moments she says, "Where was Billy today? I didn't see him."

Dunning lowers the paper again, looking at her in a way that makes her feel a chill. "What'd you say?" he asks.

"I said where was Billy. I missed seeing him."

"Billy."

Her heart jumps. She is certain he is about to say something else, something unthinkable.

"He's on A.O. today," Dunning says.

"Couldn't he switch with someone?"

"Maybe he didn't want to come," Dunning says as if bored. He goes on reading.

She cannot believe the relief even though it is something she lives on. For a moment she feels almost dizzy.

"Bud."

"What?"

"I'm going to cook dinner. Let's have a nice dinner."

"Fine," he says, lifting the bottle, tilting it up.

"What all would you like? Never mind, I'm going to surprise you."

"Don't bother about me. I'll get something at the Snack Bar."

"Why are you going to do that?"

"I have to go out anyway. I have a Rod and Gun Club meeting."

"I thought that was Wednesdays."

"This is a special one."

"Oh."

His chin is in the air as he reads something at the top of the page.

"I see they give his name today."

"I saw that," she says. "Did he have a girlfriend?"

"Maybe. I don't know."

"Somebody ought to tell her."

"She'll hear about it."

"I just wonder if anybody's going to tell her or if she'll read it in the newspaper."

"I wouldn't worry about it." He shakes the page flat to read it better.

Mayann looks at her glass. There's only a little left at the bottom of it.

"Listen, let me cook us a dinner."

"I told you. I can't."

"Can't you just skip the goddamn meeting? Call and say you won't be able to make it?"

"I'm the president," he reminds her.

She drains the glass.

"Isn't there a vice-president?"

"I have to be there."

"I guess so. I guess it'd be bad if you weren't. There wouldn't be anyone to rap the gavel or whatever you do."

He takes a swallow of beer. She goes to the refrigerator for some ice, two cubes of which she drops into her glass so he can hear it.

"I let you down."

"Nah, Cassada was the one let us down."

"It was my job to . . . Well, there's no point in going back over it. It's hard to anticipate everything."

"He couldn't cut it, that's all. It could of been worse."

"I don't see how," Isbell said.

"It could of been."

"The board's going to give us a hundred percent pilot error. Supervisory error, too."

"The weather was a big factor. Plus materiel failure. You never know."

"That's what I think they'll give."

"They may not be as tough judging as you are."

"In a way I'll be disappointed if they aren't."

"What are you talking about? The next thing you'll be committing hari-kari. These things happen. The bad thing is it happened to us. The board may clear both of us."

"Maybe. I know I could have stopped it from happening."

"Some things you can stop, some you can't. I've seen pilots get killed when a bolt wasn't safetied the way it should of been." Dunning turns his hand palm up and makes a sudden downward arc with it. "You've seen it. Hell, it's easy to second-guess. Put your ass in the cockpit and we'll see how much you know."

"You wrote to his mother, I guess."

"I'm doing that," Dunning says. "I mean I have to do that."

In the BOQ, Phipps, the summary court officer whose job it is to handle the personal effects, opens the door to Cassada's room with a strange feeling. The air in the room seems unnaturally still. He has the regular instructions plus one additional one from the major, "Tear up any love letters."

In a top drawer of the dresser he finds a benzedrine inhaler, a chit book from the club in Tripoli, flashlight batteries, shoelaces, a few coins, and a notebook. In the notebook there are details of flights and a folded IOU from a pilot in the 72nd for twenty dollars. In the lower drawers are the clothes. A flying suit and uniforms hang in the closet. As he goes through the pockets of them Phipps has a feeling like that of looking at someone while they're asleep, they might suddenly open their eyes. He has the feeling Cassada might come through the door and find him there.

An inventory of belongings has to be made. Phipps begins to mark them down on a clipboard. Shirts, six blue, five khaki. He lifts them out and tosses them onto the bed.

"What are you doing? What's going on?"

Ferguson, tall and hopeless, stands in the doorway in a flying suit.

"They made me summary court officer," Phipps says. He dropped his pencil. "I'm inventorying his things."

"Yeah, I was escort officer once."

"What's that?" Phipps says, picking up the pencil.

"You accompany the body. It's not that much fun. It was when Vandeleur was killed, before you got here. His wife was still in the States with their kid, they hadn't come over yet. When I went to the house she grabbed my hat, threw it in the street, and slammed the door. She wouldn't even talk to me. She barred me from the funeral."

He takes out a cigarette and tries to light it with the Monopol lighter that's on top of the dresser. It doesn't work. He taps it on the palm of his hand a few times and tries again. There is something about Ferguson—he is accepted, but there is a kind of invisibility that clings to him as if he's begun to paint himself out of the picture. In just a few years he will be killed in a crash at night, mistaking a dark area for a notch in the mountains near Vegas at five hundred miles an hour.

"What is there?" he says. "Anything interesting?"

In addition to the notebook there is a black address book.

"What's this?" Ferguson says, opening it and beginning to turn the pages. "Lommi. Who's that?"

"I have no idea."

"It's a Munich number. You know her?"

"Me? I'm married."

"So are a lot of people."

"Yeah, I know."

"Captain Isbell."

"Isbell?"

"Sure."

"You're kidding."

"You don't live in the BOQ. You don't know what's going on."

"He has a girlfriend in Munich?"

"A *prima* one," Ferguson says, never having seen her. "Cassada knew her."

"Is her name in that book?"

"Maybe it's Lommi. I don't know. I was asking you."

He turns the pages and the sound of it, faint, is the only sound. Phipps was with a German girl just once, in Heidelberg, before his wife came over. They stood naked together in front of the mirror. He can see it still, even now, eyes open. He can see it all the time though he cannot see it again.

"Addresses of people in Puerto Rico, looks like," Ferguson says. He comes to something inside the back cover of the book and his face becomes baffled as he reads it. "Listen to this. *Come gather for the great supper of God, to eat the flesh of kings, the flesh of captains, the flesh of mighty men . . .*"

"Say it again."

"What is it, Shakespeare?"

"It's not Shakespeare."

"Who knows what it is? Here." Ferguson hands him the address book. Phipps is reading the lines when Ferguson says, "Hey, here's something. What are you going to do with this?" He is pointing at the closet shelf.

A bottle of Puerto Rican rum, half full. Ferguson takes it and unscrews the top.

"Go ahead, take it if you want it," Phipps tells him.

"You don't want it?"

"No. Go ahead. Take it."

"Come on down when you're finished," Ferguson says, "and we'll have a blast of this." He screws the top back on. "For old Roberto. Wherever you are, pal," he says.

He leaves and Phipps sits down and goes through the address book. Most of the pages are empty. There is only that one mysterious name, the name of Isbell's girlfriend, Phipps is certain. He copies the telephone number down and reads the prophecy or vow or whatever it is again. *The flesh of captains, the flesh of mighty men.*

Among the things to be sent to the family will be a manila envelope containing the contents of the flying suit he was wearing. The address book with Lommi—she was in fact the fabric designer who lived with her mother—erased would go in there.

Two of them, well-fed, come through the inner doors and look around. The bar is empty but people are sitting at tables.

"What's it look like?" Barnes says.

"There's people here. It's OK."

"Have you been here before?"

"I don't know. Maybe. I've been to every place in town."

They sit down at a table not far in the near-darkness from a party of eight.

"Isn't anything here," Frank says, looking around for women.

"Let's have one drink."

"All right. One. I should have gone to the movie like I wanted to."

"What's wrong? Aren't you having a good time?"

"Yeah, great. It's always the same. You spend all your money and you got nothing to show for it."

"Well, you get lucky sometimes."

"They don't hang around bars. You have to meet them in the daytime."

A girl in the party looks over at them then glances away.

"I guess you're right except it's hard to get into town in the day-time."

The girl is looking. She has short hair brushed back like a boy's. After a moment she turns away again.

"Good evening," the waitress says.

"What do you want, Frank?"

"I don't want anything to drink. I'm on the early schedule."

"Coffee?" the waitress says.

"Yeah, coffee."

"I'll have a cognac," Barnes says.

"With Coke?"

"No, just cognac. What do I look like?"

"I beg your pardon?" the waitress says.

The girl is looking at him again, every time his eyes drift there. She doesn't smile. She doesn't do anything. She probably doesn't speak English.

"There's just something about them, you know?" Barnes says.

"About who?" Frank says.

"The women. I mean, you see them walking along the street, they're like horses."

"Yeah, I know. You shouldn't drink the German cognac . . ."

"Why is that?"

"Stuff'll kill you."

"It's not so bad." He is beginning to imagine her leaning over and saying something. His heart skips. The man sitting next to her turns to look and after a moment turns away. Frank has his back to them.

"You ought to stick to beer," Frank says. "They have real good beer down here. It's only half the price, too."

"I know." He feels like a frog with a light shining in his eyes.

Perhaps she's mistaking them for someone else. Finally the man touches her and she turns to him. He puts an arm around her shoulder and says something. She nods. She starts talking to the rest of them, or at least joining in, leaning on her elbows but every so often she looks over.

"The coffee's not even hot," Frank says. "What's the name of this place again?"

"The Ark."

"Remind me to steer clear of here. What are you looking at all the time?" He turns his head just as they are getting up to leave at the other table. The girl pauses for a second. She's wearing a black turtleneck sweater. Then she walks out.

"No wonder you didn't hear half of what I was saying," Frank says.

"Did you see her? I should have said something to her. I didn't have the nerve."

"Finish your drink," Frank says.

In the vestibule on the way out Frank is struggling with his coat, a big checked coat that makes him look like a German when suddenly the girl comes back in.

"Oh," she says, "I wanted to ask you something."

"Me?" Frank says, pointing at himself.

"Me," Barnes offers.

A slight intake of breath, *ja*. She nods her head. "You're not a pilot, are you?"

"Yeah, we are."

"From Furstenfeldbruck, the airfield?"

"That's right."

"Yes. I wondered. I heard planes flying over all day. You're not from the group up by Trier?"

"The 5th?"

"Yes."

"No, we're from France. Chaumont. What's your name?"

"But perhaps you know something. The other day there was an accident . . ."

"We heard about it. Two planes. The ops officer of a squadron and another guy."

"The 44th Squadron," Frank puts in.

"And were they . . . they were both killed?"

"Just one."

"Oh. Which one?"

"The wingman, I think. Why, did you know them?"

"Yes, maybe. Thank you," she says and quickly goes out.

"Hey, wait a minute!"

She is almost running to a car at the curb. As she gets in, it drives off. The two of them watch it go.

"Barnes, you're unconscious," Frank says.

"What do you mean?"

"You're just unconscious."

In the car Barnes sits with his legs doubled up in front of him, knees touching the dashboard.

"Who do you suppose she was looking for?"

"What makes you think she was looking for someone?" Frank says, turning the ignition switch. "She was looking for you, you unconscious bastard."

"No, she knew somebody. I could tell from her eyes."

"Her eyes? Is that what you noticed?"

They drive past endless blocks of apartments, every window dark. On the hidden streets there are countless others. The city is unknowable. They think they know it, they will always say they do.

"I wonder if I'll ever see her again. Probably never will."

"Who knows? With your luck . . ."

"If I wasn't expecting to, I might. Isn't that the way it always is?"

"How would I know?" Frank says.

"She looked Russian or, you know, from somewhere."

"I don't think you'll find any Russians around here."

"Way back, I mean," Barnes says.

Grace and his wife left in March, Phipps and Julie a few weeks after. Everyone went down to see them off. It was a regular thing, very much like a funeral except for the champagne. They stood around bundled against the cold, the women gossiping. Finally the train pulled out, everyone waving.

A month later it was the Isbells' turn. The grey of winter had vanished, the sky was bright. One for the road, they kept saying to him as they poured. Marian was sipping hers, talking and holding her hand over the top of the paper cup whenever someone tried to fill it, turning her head every so often to check on her children.

"Come on, Captain. One for the road."

"Yeah, one for the railroad."

Finally all the faces were looking up at them from the platform, faces they knew well and new ones that would slowly take over. So long, see you in the States. Don't be like everybody else, now; don't forget to write. A few waves and then the irrevocable, the train began to move. Isbell and his wife were waving. He held a daughter up. Marian lifted the other. They all waved.

The train went along the river, one steep bank of which was in sunshine. They sat watching the vineyards and small towns pass. Isbell felt drowsy. A warm square of sunshine was drifting across his lap. His eyes began to close. A paper cup was rolling around beneath the seat every time the train swayed a little. It hit something, lay still, then rolled back the other way.

His eyes opened sometime later when they began to slow. Coblenz, where they were to change. Marian stood up and began to put coats on the girls as the train rattled over switches. Slowly they came into the station. Marian herded the children down the aisle in front of her.

"How do you feel?" she asked, turning to Isbell.

"Thirsty."

He followed along, struggling with the bags. The platform was crowded. The car had been hot; it was different outside. The air smelled fresh. Faces bright and smiling. He took some deep breaths. The day felt better.

There was a fifteen-minute wait. Before long the train appeared, a big, blue one, the engine gleaming. The cars floated by. BREMEN EXPRESS, the plaques on them read. KÖLN, DÜSSELDORF, ESSEN, DORT-MUND, HANNOVER.

"Here it is, Daddy!" The older girl jumped up and her sister began squealing, too, waving her arms.

"I don't think this is ours."

"Here it is!" they cried.

Marian took their hands. "All right," she said, "ssh. Be still."

"Isn't it ours?" they pleaded.

"No, not yet. Are you sure?" she asked Isbell.

"Pretty sure."

"You could ask somebody."

The train was still moving past. The *Speiswagen* eased by, slowing, little chimneys on the roof, white tablecloths within. Part of the crowd moved along as it stopped, flowing to where the doors would be. A good-looking woman in her thirties got on in front of where Isbell was standing. He saw her appear in the corridor and then sit next to the window. His thoughts turned to Munich, the times there.

"Hold your daddy's hand for a minute," Marian instructed.

Isbell reached out. A small hand found his. Marian was searching in her handbag for a Kleenex.

"When will ours come, Daddy?" An adoring face was turned up towards his.

"Oh, in a few minutes. Keep your eyes peeled."

The perfect father, suitcases surrounding him, tickets in his pocket. He glanced towards the window where the woman was sitting, well-groomed and alone, as the car began to move, bearing her off. This time of year in Munich the Isar was racing under the bridges, rushing pale green, bringing the city to life. What did they feel flying down, seeing the last snow of winter in seams along the ground? Then coming in high over the blued city, the countless streets, the anticipation, the joy. They were dancing at the Palast, faces damp and youthful, streets at midnight, Sunday afternoons, the way those times the breath began to pour from her, the first *ja*. The Express was gliding faster. She was going away. *Ja. Ja. Ja!*

Not long after, the second train came, exactly on time. The enameled sign on the side of the cars read, FRANKFURT (M).

"This is ours," he said, gathering the luggage. Marian took the children's hands.

Aboard, it hardly seemed a minute before they were moving. Isbell sat watching it all for the last time. They curved through switchyards and down along the Rhine. He could see the wind blowing outside, warm and full of good things. The forked-end flags in all the river towns were waving. Couples strolled along the shore. Beneath the trees the bicyclists flashed, passing through sunlight and shade.

*I was afraid you had been killed,* she said.

*It would take more than that.*

*Who was it, then?*

*Do you remember the lieutenant who fell head over heels in love with you that night?*

*That nice one?*

*Yes.*

*Him.*

It was too soon for him to reappear, that would come years after when all of it was sacred and he had slipped in with the other romantic figures, the failed brother, the brilliant alcoholic friend, the rejected lover, the solitary boy who scorned the dance. It is only in *their* lives they die. In yours they live to the end.

The photograph Isbell remembered was of wildebeests coming down a steep embankment, hundreds of them in the dust haze that was their life, leaping, plunging into the shadowy darkness, the young ones with them, running, leaping, blood rich with excitement, among them the one who might lead one day. And in that one wild heart, everything.

*You're going back to the States, then?*

*Next month.*

*So, I don't see you again.*

*I don't know. You'll see me again.*

*No. Never.*

*Well, anyway not for a while.*

*It's hard to live like that.*

*For me, too.*

*For you it's different.*

*Ja. But you never know. Maybe sometime.*

*Good-bye, Tommy.*

The river was wide. On it the boats were moving, the big white sightseeing boats, the side-wheelers and barges. Memories seemed reflected from the shining water.

"Are you sleepy, dear?" Marian asked.

"What? No. Just thinking."

"I guess we're going to miss it."

"Yes."

It was all passing, for the first time as well as the last. His eyes devoured everything yet hardly made things out. He did not know what he was thinking. It all seemed a long struggle which he could not decide if he'd won or lost. Parts of it he could hardly remember. The rest was still clear. But it was all back, falling behind. There was no use trying to save anything. After a while you began to understand that. In the end you got on a train and went along the river.

Printed in the United States
by Baker & Taylor Publisher Services